ABOVE & BEYOND

DON'T MISS THESE ALEX ANDER THRILLERS!

Alex Ander writes what he enjoys reading – action thrillers packed with fistfights, gunfights, good-and-decent main characters, and heart-pounding excitement and adventure...all with clean language, no graphic sex, and an undertone of faith from a Christian worldview.

Aaron Hardy – Ex-Special Forces

The Unsanctioned Patriot

American Influence

Deadly Assignment

Patriot Assassin

The Nemesis Protocol

Necessary Means

Foreign Soil

Of Patriots and Tyrants

Act of Justice

The Last Kill

Two Minutes to War

Three Days in Rome

Dark Days of the Republic

Act of War

BIG SKY Series – Sheriff Wade Lockhart

Big Sky

Ambush

Reckoning

Jacob St. Christopher – Former FBI Hostage Rescue
Protect & Defend
Word of Honor
A Vow to the Innocent
Above & Beyond
Hard Road to Redemption

Jaxon Reigns – Ex-CIA Paramilitary Operations
To Reign Supreme
Hard Reign

Special Agent Cruz – FBI Agent
Vengeance is Mine
Defense of Innocents
Plea for Justice

Jessica Devlin – U.S. Marshal
Trust Fall
No Good Options
Let the Hunt Begin

Other Action Thrillers
Kill Order
Far From Mercy
Executive One Foxtrot

FREE Ebook
Escape & Evade
Go to AlexAnderNovelist.com

ABOVE & BEYOND

A HOSTAGE RESCUE THRILLER

ALEX ANDER

This book is a work of fiction. All names, characters, places and incidents are the products of the author's imagination or are used fictitiously. Any similarities to real events or locations or actual persons, living or dead, is entirely coincidental.

TABLE OF CONTENTS

*"For the Son of Man did not come to be served,
but to serve and to give his life
as a ransom for many."*

—Mark, Chapter 10: Verse 45

ABOVE & BEYOND

JULY 21ST; 11:11 P.M.
UPSTATE NEW YORK

Stockwell ducked under a roundhouse right and came up before ducking again, under a wild left. The five-eleven, FBI special agent thrust the heel of her black tactical boot into a muscle-shirted man's gut.

The air leaving his lungs, Muscle Shirt doubled over and hugged his belly.

Stockwell sent out two right jabs, rocking MS's head backward, before connecting with a left cross. The communication device in her ear crackled.

"Stockwell, I heard gunfire. What's your situation?"

She spun around and struck her opponent with a wheel kick to his right ear, propelling him into a wall.

"Deanna!"

"Now's..." looking down, "not..." she scanned the floor, searching for her Glock 19M, knocked from her hands during an earlier scuffle, "a good time, Jake." She saw movement in her peripheral vision—a second man, pistol in hand, had entered the garage.

MS shook his head back and forth, clearing cobwebs.

Abandoning the hunt for her gun, Stockwell sidestepped left, grabbed a crescent wrench from the

ALEX ANDER   1

workbench, whacked MS in the head and hurled the tool at the armed newcomer, hitting him in the sternum.

Newcomer grunted and clutched his chest. A second later, he lifted his weapon.

Stockwell's eyes grew bigger. *Oh crap.* The leather jacket and blue jean clad woman whirled around, took three running steps and threw herself across the hood of an older model Chevrolet Impala. She slid over the left fender, rolled, and landed on her left hip, her hands absorbing part of the impact.

Incoming bullets blew out car windows and poked holes in the sheet metal.

On her butt, her back against the driver's door, hunching shoulders, she covered the ponytail knot at the back of her head, as glass pellets blanketed her.

The shooting stopped. A second later, something hollow bounced off the floor a couple times and settled.

She lifted her head. *Reload.* Stockwell rolled onto her belly and placed flat hands on the concrete. At eye level with the floor, she examined the smooth, gray surface. Her ears picked up the sound of metal scraping against metal.

She whipped her head right and glimpsed an empty magazine in front of two brown work boots. *Out of time, Dee.* Coming back to the left, Stockwell spotted the Glock—slide locked to the rear—under the Chevy's front bumper. She jumped to her feet and ran along the vehicle's driver side in a low crouch.

Gunfire commenced.

She grabbed a spare magazine from the pouch on her left hip and stretched out her right arm under the Impala's front end.

Jacketed bullets skipped off the hood.

Seeing sparks, she flinched before thrusting out her hand. Getting fingertips on the Glock's polymer grip, she lifted her gaze.

MS wobbled toward her, swiping at the bloody gash on his temple.

Stockwell gaped at his looming, muscled figure.

Newcomer let off the trigger, as his partner entered his line of sight.

She curled her fingers, her nails bringing the Glock closer.

MS towered over her.

She grabbed the gun, rolled onto her back and brought knees to chest.

Reaching for his female combatant, MS dove forward.

The soles of her boots met with his pectoral muscles, as she continued the backward somersault. Halfway into the roll, she did a leg press.

MS somersaulted over her and crashed into a red, waist-high toolbox on wheels. The metal carrier tipped over. MS came down hard.

On her back, Stockwell thumbed the magazine release, rammed a full mag home, ran the slide forward and lifted her head and shoulders. Acquiring a flash sight picture on Newcomer's chest, she got off three, quick shots.

His body convulsed before twisting out of sight on the other side of the Chevy.

Going flat again, she lifted the pistol over her head, and saw an upside down view of MS.

On his feet, clutching a ball peen hammer, his frame coiled in a low crouch, he sprang toward her.

Stockwell's trigger finger twitched three times.

Three bullets struck MS, two in the chest, one in the forehead. His body seized. His head lolled backward, as he dropped to his knees and fell over sideways.

Rolling onto her left shoulder, she brought her weapon to bear on Newcomer.

From just beyond the right front tire, his dull eyes gawked back at her.

She waited another moment.

He never blinked.

After a final glance behind her to verify the other assailant's motionless status, Stockwell laid her head on the floor and emptied her lungs in one rush. "Jake, it's me." She huffed twice. "Garage's clear." Taking her finger off the Glock's trigger, she grabbed more oxygen. "The Innocents?"

"Negative...still searching." Silence passed between them. "You okay?"

Standing, "A little winded..." she swapped out the

partial magazine for her last full one, "but I'm good." The sound of a piece of paper slapping against a hard surface drew her attention.

"Copy that. Almost done here…"

She looked toward the far corner of the garage and saw a full-size, full-color poster of a woman in a pink, two-piece bikini, a large wrench in one hand and the thumb of the other pulling up on the side tie of her G-string.

Stockwell approached the banner. Bullets from Newcomer's pistol had punctured the paper woman's body. The edges of the paper flapped. She holstered her weapon and put a hand to the hole on the woman's thigh; a faint draft wafted over her palm.

"…meet me at the back door, Stockwell."

She tore the tall picture in half widthwise, "Copy that," and frowned at a small door set flush with the wall. "I need to check out something first. Give me a minute." She dug her nails into one of the cracks around the panel and tugged. The rectangle moved enough for her to get fingers into the one-inch gap. Drawing her Glock and Pelican 2350 flashlight, Stockwell took a step back, swung open the section of wall and eyed a wooden hatch, secured by a barrel bolt.

She undid the locking mechanism, pulled on the secret access door and aimed her light and pistol toward a darkened opening; a pungent odor greeted her. After covering her nose with the back of her wrist, and inhaling, she lit up the small cubicle. Her eyes grew wide and she lowered the Glock. *Oh my...*

. . .

"All right...be careful, Stockwell." Wearing a black leather jacket, black jeans and black tactical boots, Jacob St. Christopher had cleared the main level of the house. His Coonan 1911-style 357 Magnum in both hands and pointed toward the upstairs walkway, a wall on either side of him, he ascended the stairs to the upper level. Thirteen steps later, his forward boot touched down on the second floor carpeting.

Straight ahead, ten feet away, was the bathroom; it appeared empty. He leaned right and aimed his 1911 left, at a bedroom next to the bathroom; it was dark. He continued listing, until he peeked around the wall on his left and saw a second and third room. Exposed to incoming fire from four directions, his heart rate spiked, as he sidestepped toward the bath.

Clearing the bathroom, he darted into the bedroom next to it. His eyes adjusted to the darkness and he cleared the room. Coming to the doorway again, he swayed left and looked down the short hallway. *Two down...two to go.*

Jacob crossed the hall again to get a better angle on room number two. With his 357 pointed at the blackness ahead, he kept his eyes trained on the last room at his nine o'clock. He spotted movement a split second before hearing the reports.

     ABOVE & BEYOND

Several projectiles zipped by his nose; one shattered a bathroom mirror.

He charged into the room straight ahead for cover. His back against the door, he surveyed the space and found nobody. Another string of fire chewed up the wooden doorjamb to his left. He brought his shoulder up and turned away from flying splinters. "Homeland Security. Drop your weapon and come out with your hands up."

Foul language preceded a third round of nine-millimeter projectiles slamming into the wood above his shoulder.

"Okay, if that's the way you want it...I can play hardball too." Jacob stole a peak at his 1911, thinking of the more powerful 357 Magnums in the gun. "But my balls are bigger than yours." He burst into the last bedroom, sending 158-grain jacketed hollow points toward his adversary.

Passing the archway, he dove, rolled and came to a kneeling position. In a glance, he took in the room layout: bed directly in front of him, closet door on his two o'clock and two armoires against the twelve o'clock wall. The assailant was nowhere in sight. Jacob dropped to his right shoulder, aimed the Coonan at an ankle in the gap between the bed and the carpet, and fired once.

The aggressor screamed.

Jacob leaped to his feet, rounded the bed and put the 1911's front sight on the man's nose. "Hands! Show me your hands!"

Yelling, clutching his blown-out ankle, and his weapon, the man glared at Jacob.

Jacob met the writhing man's stare. After sneaking a peek at the accoster's Taurus 92 pistol, he shook his head at his adversary. "Don't do it. You're dead if you do."

The man propped himself on one elbow and put a knee onto the floor.

"I said, don't—" Jacob took a step and drove his boot into the man's nose.

Falling backward, the assailant swung the Taurus forward.

Jacob stomped on the wrist, pinning the gun to the floor. He planted his right knee in the man's chest and punched him repeatedly.

The kidnapper's head bounced off the floor five times. He opened his hand, and the pistol slid onto the carpeting.

After tossing the offending weapon onto the bed, Jacob grabbed a leather belt from one of the armoires and bound the man's hands behind his back. "The next time I tell you," he secured the criminal to a leg on the bedframe, "to drop your weapon—" he turned an ear toward the sound of a revving engine. Hurrying to the window, he threw back the curtains and saw headlights near a pole barn at the back of the property. "Son-of-a—"

Snatching the gun from the mattress, Jacob bolted out of the bedroom, and bounded down the stairs. The front door was two steps from the bottom of the staircase. He crashed through the open door he had entered earlier, jumped off the porch and ran to the middle of the driveway.

Lighting him up, the car's headlights were basketballs, growing bigger by the second.

Jacob stood his ground. He exchanged the partial magazine in the Coonan for a fresh seven-rounder and aimed his gun at the windshield. His instinct was to aim for the driver. Go for the kill shot. He squeezed the Coonan tighter, only to relax a little. *What if the kids are in there?* He pointed the weapon at the front grille. *Shoot the radiator. Disable the car, Jake.* He bobbed his eyebrows and jerked his head to the side. *And hope I'm not run over in the process.*

The headlights now seemed the size of inflatable exercise balls.

Jacob frowned. *Would he bother to take the kids with him?*

The two headlights merged into one massive beam.

He lifted the Coonan toward the windshield. *No, he wouldn't have time to mess around with them.* He lowered the Coonan. *Can't take the chance.* He closed his left eye and applied pressure to the trigger.

In his ear: "Jake, I found the kids. They're safe."

Thank God. Jacob emptied his Magnum at the windshield, reloaded and sent four more rounds downrange.

The speeding car's front end lurched to Jacob's left before the rear end swerved in the opposite direction. The tires gained traction, and the vehicle lunged forward, missing him by a few feet.

Jacob saw the driver through the open side window; his head was back against the headrest.

Seconds later, the older model Caprice slammed into a large oak tree in the front yard. The hood folded into the letter 'A.' The horn blared above a hissing sound. Smoke billowed out from the engine compartment.

"Jake, are you all right?"

Jacob approached the driver side, gun pointed at the driver.

His face bloodied, the man behind the wheel was still.

After a few moments, Jacob reached into the vehicle and pulled the man's head back, stopping the horn from sounding. Observing three bullet wounds—two in the chest and one through the Adam's apple—he checked for a pulse, but only as a formality.

"Jake, talk to me. Where are you?"

"All good, Stockwell. I'm in the front yard." Observing the dead man, he saw movement in his peripheral vision and pivoted his head toward a slim figure.

Stockwell emerged from the garage, next to the house, carrying a frail girl in one arm and holding hands with a boy, a couple years older than his sister.

Following a last look at the corpse, Jacob left the

          ABOVE & BEYOND

carnage behind and met his partner and the kids at the house, holstering his Coonan during the walk. Noticing deep lines on her forehead, and a frown, he flashed an upturned thumb, "I'm okay," before going to one knee and smiling at the boy. "Hey there little man."

The boy drew nearer to his female protector.

"My name's Jacob." He held out his hand. "Pleased to meet you, son. My friends..."

The youngster hid behind Stockwell.

"...call me..." he wavered and half whispered his next word, "Jake."

The boy peeked out from around her left leg.

Jacob snickered. "That's okay, Timothy. I wouldn't trust me either." He stood and regarded his girlfriend. The strained look on her face had been replaced by the beautiful one he loved.

Stockwell stopped bouncing little Annabelle up and down, reached behind her and cupped the back of Timothy's head. "It's okay, Timmy. He's with me. You don't have to be afraid." She came back to Annabelle. "Isn't that right, Annie?" She tapped the little girl's nose, "Boop."

Biting down on her index finger, the toddler smiled, rocked forward and put her head on the woman's shoulder.

After another minute of playing with the kids, Stockwell eyed her man.

Jacob beamed.

Her eyebrows came together before she mimicked his gesture. "What is it?"

He shook his head. "Oh nothing."

She squinted at him. "I know that look, Mr. St. Christopher. You have something to say. So say it."

Chuckling, he glanced at Annabelle and Timothy before coming back to her. "It's just," a twinkle materialized in his eye, "I think you'd make a terrific mom, you know that?"

She barely turned her head and half closed an eye at him. A split-second later, "Oh no you don't," she shook her head. "No, no...I see what you're doing here."

He showed her his palms and pretended to mope. "What am I doing?"

"You're trying to sweet talk me. I told you I wasn't interested in having kids, remember?"

Timothy had mustered the courage to stand next to Stockwell, beneath his sister, hugging his rescuer's right leg.

Snickering, studying the sidewalk that led to the front door, Jacob cozied up to his woman. "You're only thirty-one."

"So."

"So..." he wrapped his right arm around her shoulders and gave her a playful grin, "I still have time to work on you, wear you down."

"Is that your strategy?" She spied his slowly approaching lips. "You should know," she peeked at his eyes, "I don't wear down that easily." Her attention zipped back to his mouth.

"That's okay. I love a good challenge." He squeezed her shoulder and kissed her. "But you won't be able to resist me for long, Miss Stockwell."

She sniggered and kissed him a second time.

"See? My charm's working already." He glimpsed her lips. "You came back for seconds."

THREE HOURS LATER
JULY 22ND; 2:12 A.M.
NEW YORK CITY

The bride-to-be slammed her shot glass onto the table, swallowed, stamped her feet on the floor and let out a short scream before slouching into the couch. Her bridesmaids chuckled and shook their heads before returning their drinks to the table.

Ayda listed toward the inebriated woman and gave her a one-armed hug. "Belle...girl...you're drunk. I think we should go."

Clutching Ayda's face in her hands, "Mmm..." Belle planted a kiss on her friend's lips, "aah. You're," her words were slurred, "sweet, but, I...I...I," she hesitated, "what was I saying? Oh yeah...I'm not drunk. I...I love you."

Standing, tugging on Belle, Ayda glanced at her twin sister, "Give me a hand, Zoe," before coming back to Belle, "We know. We know. We love you too. Come on girl." She grabbed one arm "Let's get..."

Zoe took the other limb.

"...you home." Together, the twins hoisted the star of the bachelorette party to her feet. "It's time—" grunting, Ayda took a wide step to steady her friend's teetering frame, "we call this party," she repositioned Belle's bodyweight, "and this night...over."

"But I thought...I thought you," Belle lolled her head to the other side to see Zoe, "*and you*...were my friends, my peeps, my gal pals. I thought we," she burped, "we were going to...to party until the early...morning hours." She hiccupped. "Excuse me. I—I think I burped. Excuse me." A moment passed. "Isn't anybody going to...excuse me?"

Ayda patted Belle's shoulder. "You're excused, sweetie. Now just keep putting one foot in front of the other. Zo Zo and I will do the steering." To the backdrop of lights flashing, music playing and people dancing, the twins navigated Belle through the crowded nightclub.

. . .

Outside the club, the trio shuffled along the street, heading for Ayda's car. Nightlife was still bustling at this hour, as partygoers hurried from one bar to another. Honking car horns, and shouts from drivers, were the sounds of the night.

Zoe slowed.

Ayda looked left, across Belle's sagging body, at her sister. "What is it?"

"Your car's," Zoe motioned, "just down that alley."

"Nope." Ayda shook her head. "Not going to happen."

"Come on." Zoe lifted her friend a little higher and re-situated the girl's arm around her neck. "She's getting heavy. I don't want to do this for another three blocks."

"It's not safe." Ayda took a step, but stopped when her sister did not move with her.

"Just this once." Zoe raised her foot. "These heels are already killing me."

Ayda glanced at her own spike-heeled pumps, her ankles turning out slightly under Belle's weight. She looked ahead, knowing their intended route, the longer route, the safer route, would mean a couple blisters in the morning. Noting the time of day in her head, she chuckled inwardly. *Okay...later today.*

Older by one minute and fifty-eight seconds than her sibling, Ayda might as well had been born ten years earlier. She was the mature one, the sensible one. She was the one who only had two drinks in the last six hours.

Zoe was carefree and laid back. She lived for the here and now, never thinking too far ahead. Having a vibrant smile and attitude that attracted people, she was the popular kid in school. She was fun. She was the one everyone else wanted to be around, to emulate.

Even though they were identical twins, physically, Ayda and Zoe's personalities were as far apart as the first letters in their names were.

Ayda gave the alley another long look. *Seems empty.* Her grip slipping, she grunted and hefted Belle's body higher. A short, stiff breeze blew down the sidewalk and up her tight-fitting skirt. She shivered, while eyeing the darkened stretch of concrete.

"I saw that." Zoe pulled the threesome toward the

alley. "You're just as tired as I am."

Biting her lower lip, Ayda glimpsed her sister, "You know," before changing course, "that's always been your problem…shortcuts…you love taking them."

The women headed down the lonely alley.

Zoe rolled her eyes. "Lay off, will you? This was supposed to be a fun night out. If I'd wanted a lecture, I would've stayed home and talked with Mom."

"I'm just saying," Ayda shot a nervous glance over her shoulder toward the dimly lit space behind a dumpster, "if you focused more on your future, instead of what's at your feet, you—"

"Blah, blah, blah…" feeling a jolt of adrenaline, the younger sister picked up her pace, "fulfill my potential, make something of my life…I've heard it all before."

"Hey, I'm—"

"Just trying to look out for me?" Zoe confronted Ayda. "Teach me? Guide me? Thanks, but I have a mother for that. I don't need another one."

"As your sister, I'm just—"

"That's right. Did you ever think of being *my sister* for just one," she cursed, "moment?" She faced forward. "Whatever the hell happened to you, Ay?" Ay was Zoe's nickname for Ayda. "We had a blast growing up…you and me. We did some crazy stuff together. And then you," she wavered, "you just got *old* on me…overnight."

Ayda felt heat building in her face and neck. "Well," she barked, "*one of us* had to grow up."

Zoe whipped her head toward her sister, her mind flipping through several foul words. She settled on something else. "Bite me."

Ayda locked eyes with Zoe for several seconds.

Somewhere down the alley, a bottle rolled across the pavement.

Both women looked backward.

"What," Zoe's voice cracked, "was that?"

After a brief pause, the glass container rolled again before the atmosphere turned quiet.

"It," squinting, Ayda studied the darker corners of the dimly lit backstreet, "it...was probably just a stray cat. Let's get to the car."

. . .

Following a long and silent one-minute walk, the threesome came to a parking lot.

"You've got to be kidding me." Ayda scowled at the narrow space between a van and the driver side of her car. "Jerk." She took Belle's arm from around her neck, and the siblings leaned their friend against the trunk of Ayda's vehicle. The elder sister fumbled through her purse before retrieving keys. She tapped the 'unlock' button, illuminating her car's interior.

The van's side door opened.

Ayda and Zoe turned their heads toward the noise.

Wearing clown masks, two men leaped out and rushed toward the female trio.

Zoe opened her mouth to scream, but a 'Clown'

forced a black hood over her head, muting her cries.

Gaping at the second Clown, Ayda shoved a hand back into her purse, searching for the pepper spray she carried. Her fingers touched the smooth canister.

Clown 2 threw a hood over her head, knocked the purse from her hands and tossed her into the vehicle. Two more pairs of hands clutched her ankles and dragged her, feet first, over rough carpeting.

The manhandling bunched her skirt around her waist. Ayda winced, as the carpet's coarse fabric burned her hip. While two men bound her hands and feet, she sensed another body land next to her. *Zoe? Belle?*

The door slammed shut and the van sped away.

Feeling her chest tightening, Ayda arched her back, but her lungs remained empty. She shut her eyes. *Calm down. Just...calm...down. Focus on that first breath. Just get one.* She slowly inhaled through her nose. The burning sensation subsided. *That's it. You can do this.* She grabbed a little more oxygen. *Fight it, Ayda. Fight it. Don't let it take over.*

CHAPTER 3
MOTHER NATURE

Propping herself on one elbow, Stockwell trained an ear in the direction of the bed's headboard, the wall inches away, and ultimately, the source of the noise on the opposite side. She flopped onto her back and rubbed her eyes with the heels of her hands. She kicked off the covers, revealing bare legs below purple, low-rise lace women's boy shorts. A white, midriff t-shirt exposed a flat stomach. She let out a long yawn, stretched four limbs and ran fingers through long blonde hair before scratching her scalp.

After another few minutes of listening to the muffled sound, grinning the entire time, she slid out of bed, padded across the carpet, and into the hallway. Stopping at the door across from her bedroom, eavesdropping, her grin growing wider, she swayed her head from side to side. *I love that song, but I didn't know he did.* Unable to resist the temptation any longer, she rapped on the wooden door.

. . .

Jacob stood in front of the sink, from waist to knees, a white towel hung around his naked six-two, two hundred pound build. He drew the safety razor down a cheek and plunged the cutting tool into the water-filled basin. He took a deep breath and his voice climbed a couple octaves for the next verse.

Swishing the blades in the water, he turned his head to the side and planned the next attack on the stubble.

Someone knocked on the door.

He listed right, opened the door and smiled. "Hey."

Her right shoulder against the doorjamb, arms folded across bare skin between her shirt and shorts, Stockwell pivoted into the bathroom. "Hey."

Jacob rotated the volume dial to the left. "The music didn't wake you, did it?"

"No," she glimpsed the dark hair, spreading over his muscular chest, "*the music* didn't wake me." Her gaze settled on his rugged jaw, gray eyes and the wet, disheveled, jet-black hair on his head. "However, I *was* wondering if you had a cat you failed to tell me about."

He peeped at her long legs, crossed at the ankle, and t-shirt. His gaze lingered a half second at the breasts lifting the skimpy top's front hem a couple inches away from her body.

Noticing the lack of focus, she inwardly smiled. *My eyes are up here, Jake.*

Making eye contact, he frowned. "A cat? What do you mean?"

She raised a corner of her mouth. "I thought maybe the poor thing had gotten its tail stepped on, or something."

After glancing at the radio, Jacob chortled and faced her. "That bad, huh?"

"I'm kidding. You have the voice of an angel." She poked her chin at the music player. "That's the second Anne Murray song in a row," she paused, "so I know you're not listening to a station."

"Nope." Averting his attention from the thin cotton material, covering most of her torso, he grabbed a plastic CD case and handed it to her. Jacob glimpsed the towel around his lower body. *Going to be hard to keep Mother Nature from making an appearance in this.*

Stockwell eyed a picture of the artist on the cover. "So do all Army Rangers and FBI SWAT guys listen to Anne Murray?"

"Only the ones with good taste."

She laughed. "And those not afraid of being teased."

"Hey," Jacob held out his hands a little ways, palms up, pinching the razor between thumb and forefinger. "At thirty-five, I've experienced a lot of bad..." looking away, he recalled his time in war zones in Afghanistan, and FBI raids on American soil, "*bad* stuff." His eyes dipped toward the CD player. "Having my 'man card' called into question over liking her music," he came back to Stockwell and shook his head, "doesn't even move the needle."

"Yeah," she set the case on the sink, her mind drifting toward her own horrifying, job-related stories, "I suppose it wouldn't." She took a breath and blew out the air in one, soft puff. "So...I just wanted to thank you again for letting me stay here."

"No problem. How was your bed? Sleep well?" Jacob scraped the razor over his cheeks a few times.

"I did. It was good...comfy." She watched him remove the white foam from his neck, revealing clear skin.

"Any idea on," flattening his upper lip, his voice changing as a result, "when you'll," he shaved below his nose, "be able to move back into your place?" After Jacob had shot an assassin in her bathroom, Stockwell had asked to stay at his home, while a restoration company cleaned her apartment.

Watching him rinse the shaver, she flashed a sheepish grin. "Well...speaking of that...since you asked..."

He trimmed the hard-to-get areas and splashed water on his face.

"...my place is actually," she wavered, "all done."

Jacob patted his skin with a hand towel and threaded the cloth through a ring, anchored to the wall. "That's great." Out of the corner of his eye, he saw her shoulders sag a bit, while fiddling with the pump on the bottle of hand soap. "Isn't it?"

"Well," she flicked her eyes his way before going back to staring at the soap bottle, "yes...yes it is." She stood tall, cupped and arched her back, making her breasts appear even bigger, and did small side bends, stretching stiff muscles.

It took all of Jacob's inner strength to concentrate on his temporary roommate's eyes.

"I suppose I," she flashed a pathetic, disappearing smile, "can go back home tonight."

"You don't sound very excited." He did a one-eighty, leaned back against the vanity and crossed arms and ankles. "Is everything all right, Stockwell?"

Folding hands around her mouth and nose, she studied the floor, while ambling further into the room, away from him. With each step, her warm, bare feet stuck to the tile.

Losing restraint, Jacob ogled her slender figure, slowing a bit when he came to the gentle angle of her underwear's hem, which showed him a sliver of the start of two butt cheeks. "You can tell me anything. You know that, right?"

She spun around and aimed her praying hands at him. "I don't think I'm ready to go back there," she hesitated, "after what happened. I...I keep seeing his body every time I go in there to pee. Sorry," she put one hand on her hip and held her forehead with the other, "too much information."

He chuckled before pushing off from the sink, clutching her upper arms and giving her a warm smile. "Deanna..."

She looked up at him.

"...you can stay here for as long as you want."

Her mood lightened. "Are you sure? I don't want to

be a burden."

He slid his hands under her shirtsleeves and gently squeezed her soft skin. "You're definitely not a burden. In fact, consider," he bobbed his head backward, toward the bedroom across the hall, "*that room...your room* from now on."

"What about Mandy?" Jacob and Stockwell had saved Mandy—Amanda Applegate—from a Mafioso. The teenager was now in the care of Jacob, and his ex-wife, and living at his ex-wife's home.

"I'll take the couch when she stays over. She can have my bed." He lifted a shoulder. "Don't worry. It'll all work out."

Rising to tiptoes and draping her chin over his shoulder, Stockwell embraced him. "I can't tell you how much this means to me. I was *so* dreading going home tonight."

Wrapping one arm around her, Jacob drew her to himself and sunk the fingers of his free hand into the hair cascading down her back. His gaze shifted from her arched lower back to the opposite curves beneath the purple boy shorts. "It's no problem." He kissed the crook of her neck. "I like having you here." He shot another look at her lace underwear. *I really like having you here.*

She smiled and hugged him tighter. Moments later, she felt something inch across her shorts. Her eyes grew wider and her brows soared higher. Taking a step backward, she glanced at his towel, looked up and spied his flushed cheeks. Giving him a straight-lined grin, while motioning toward the door, "I should probably go," she took a step in the same direction. "I'll shower when you're—"

"No." He took her by the elbow. "Don't go."

Spinning around, she squared her body with his.

He watched her hair fly over her shoulder and cover the t-shirt over her right breast. He admired her blue eyes. "Please," his voice was deeper, softer, "stay...take your shower."

Stepping closer to him, her tone and volume matching his, "Are you sure that's..." she focused on his lips, "what you want?" She laid hands on his chest and tipped her head back a little ways.

Cupping her lower back with both hands, he pulled. "I've never been so sure," he kissed her, "of anything," another kiss, "in my whole life."

Stockwell put a hand on either side of his neck and caressed his lips with hers. "Well if it means that much to you..."

He felt her warm breath on his chin.

"...then," she lightly touched her mouth to his before pulling away a fraction of an inch, "I guess..."

He inhaled the mild scent of her perfume, a fruity blend.

"...I'll have to take that shower."

Touching his nose to hers, he grinned and ran his hands over her smooth skin, under the back of her shirt.

"I don't think that's what either one of us is talking about right now."

"Oh, I know exactly what we're talking about." She felt more movement outside of her underwear. "But if I don't get in that shower, this might end up going where we both agreed *not* to go," a beat, "at least not right away."

Recalling their conversation, from a while ago, at Joe Allen Restaurant, Jacob shut his eyes and lowered his forehead to hers. They had agreed not to rush into the sexual aspect of their relationship. Stockwell wanted to take time to date him, get to know him first. His chest swelled and he blew a long breath down the front of her body. "You're right."

She took his head in her hands and gave him an innocent peck. "I love you, Jacob."

After removing his hands from under the back of her shirt, "I love you, too, Stockwell," he scooped his phone off the sink and pivoted toward the door. "Oh...I almost forgot." He wagged his phone at her, while backing out of the bathroom. "Higs called."

Stockwell placed a fresh towel and washcloth near the shower.

Jacob grabbed the doorknob. "He wants to see us at the Keep right away this morning."

"The Keep?"

"It's what I started calling the office building...on Staten Island. The thing reminds me of a castle keep. It's fortified with all kinds of technology."

Standing tall, she faced him, hugged herself and pulled up her shirt. "Did he say what," she yanked the garment back down, "*oops*," after stopping just shy of giving him a show. "Sorry..." she flashed an awkward grin, "wasn't thinking."

Jacob smirked. "No need to apologize."

She tipped her head to one side, a thin smile on her face. "No?"

"I wouldn't have been the least bit offended."

After a quick snicker, she righted her head and jutted out her chin toward the cell phone. "Did Higs say what he wanted?"

Retreating, "He said he'd tell us when we got there," Jacob pulled the door shut.

Standing in the hallway, his back to the bathroom, envisioning her figure, he glimpsed his towel and sighed. *This is going to be one heck of an exercise in self-control.* A moment later, he set his jaw. *You can do it, Jake. You're a Ranger. You've fought tougher battles...and won.* Shaking his head, inwardly chuckling, "The trouble is," he mumbled under his breath, "this is one fight I wouldn't mind *losing.*"

ABOVE & BEYOND

9:16 A.M.
STATEN ISLAND, NEW YORK
ST. GEORGE NEIGHBORHOOD
NONDESCRIPT OFFICE BUILDING "THE KEEP"

At the far end of a conference table, Jacob pushed a white rook two squares, "Check," while hearing the tail end of Stockwell's phone conversation over his shoulder.

"Thank you, Agent Curtis." Outside the room, Stockwell paced. "I appreciate the information. Let me know if anything changes."

Standing on the opposite side of a black-and-red-checkered board, facing Jacob, Higs slid his king over one space.

Jacob picked up his bishop and placed it next to his rook.

Alfred "Higs" Higginbottom, arms crossed over his chest, patted his pursed lips with an index finger. His hair was an even mix of black and gray strands. Gold, wire-rimmed circular spectacles rested on his nose. He wore a crisp white shirt with no tie, black pants and black Oxfords. Higs glimpsed his opponent.

Jacob met his employer's gaze.

The fifty-three-year-old brought his knight closer to

his king. "You're doing quite well, Mr. St. Christopher."

Jacob nodded. "It's been a while, but I still remember how to play." He moved his queen. "Check."

"Thanks again, Agent Curtis." Stockwell entered the small conference room. "Okay," she took her place at the table, "I just got an update on the kids. Annabelle and Timothy have been examined by doctors and are back with their parents. Both are doing very well, considering the circumstances."

Jacob sat at the table and crossed his legs, ankle on knee. "That's great news. Anyone say how they're doing, psychologically?"

She turned up her palms. "It's too early to tell." The children had been kidnapped and held in a small, secret room in a garage for five days before Stockwell discovered them.

Higs moved a chess piece and joined them, sitting at the head of the table, Jacob on his right. "At this early juncture, the most important thing to consider is the youngster's healthy physical well-being." He swung a finger back and forth between his employees. "For which, both of you have earned much-deserved praise."

Jacob eyed Stockwell across the table from him. "Allow me to translate. I'm becoming more fluent in speaking *Higs* these days. He says...job well done."

She smiled.

"So," Jacob faced his boss, "what's going on, Higs? Why the urgent need to meet this morning?" He gestured toward Stockwell. "We were supposed to have the day off."

His forehead wrinkling, Higs took a big breath and exhaled. "Early this morning, I received a phone call from a good friend of mine, Paul Gentry. We go back to my college days. We both earned degrees in computer science. I went to work for the government, while he chose the private sector."

Stockwell crossed her legs under the table, leaned back in her chair and placed folded hands on her lap.

"He eventually started his own software firm, which became quite successful. Perhaps you've heard of it...Gentry Security Solutions."

Jacob shook his head. "Can't say that I have."

Stockwell mimicked her man. "Me neither."

"Their software," continued Higs, "protects dozens of Fortune 500 companies." He removed his glasses, shut his eyes and pinched the bridge of his nose for the next several moments.

Jacob exchanged a look with Stockwell, who shrugged and cocked her head to one side.

"At any rate," Higs put on his spectacles, "I did not summon you here this morning for a history lesson. Mr. Gentry has two daughters—twins—Ayda and Zoe. I've had the honor of attending many of their special celebrations: baptism, first communion, high school graduation, sporting ev—" Higs made a face and rubbed his brow before gathering his composure a few seconds later.

Stockwell leaned forward. "Are you all right, Higs?"

"The night before last, both Ayda and Zoe were kidnapped from a parking lot in New York City."

Jacob planted both feet on the floor and rocked forward. "What?"

"They had been out celebrating with a friend...a bachelorette party if you will. A young woman, Belle, is to be married soon."

"Was she abducted too?"

Higs shook his head. "No. She was left at the scene, unharmed...shaken, but unharmed."

"Did she get a look at those who took her friends?"

"She said there were two men, both of whom wore masks...clown faces. The incident happened quickly. The young lady only saw a dark-colored van; no license plate number, no make or model."

"Obviously," Stockwell interjected, "the police are involved, right?"

Higs nodded. "Yes; however, the FBI has usurped the case. According to Paul—excuse me...Mr. Gentry—the FBI is following standard protocol for these matters."

"Has there been any contact from the kidnappers, any ransom demands?"

"Yes." Higs turned stoic again. "A hefty sum of money was demanded. And if that demand is not met..." his voice trailed off.

Everyone in the room knew the ending to that

sentence.

"Did the kidnappers," his voice low and even, "give a," *deadline*, Jacob hesitated, "date and time, Higs?"

"Ten o'clock...tonight. Paul is getting the money ready. I'm searching databases for any clues that may help locate Ayda and Zoe's whereabouts. And I understand the FBI is doing everything in its power; however," the troubled man eyed Stockwell and Jacob, "I would be most grateful if the two of you—"

"Done." Jacob checked the time on his watch. "We have almost twelve-and-a-half hours. Where do we start?"

Higs faced Stockwell.

She smiled and touched his forearm. "Whatever you need from us."

He gave her a straight-lined smile. "Thank you. I've sent all available information on this case to your phones...as well as personal information on the Gentrys. May I suggest speaking with the parents and Belle to ascertain details from their perspective?"

Rising from his chair, "I take it..." Jacob motioned toward Stockwell.

She had her phone out, scrolling through the data from Higs.

"...their address is in—"

"I have it right here." She stood. "Paul and Lisa Gentry live upstate...about two hours from here."

Jacob came back to Higs. "I'd like to take the truck."

The older man lifted hands. "All resources are at your

disposal."

"Thanks. You ready Stockwell? You need to get anything?"

"No. I'm good."

Higs followed his people out of the conference room and to the elevator, a short distance away. "There is one more thing. After my wife was murdered, Paul and I had many discourses about law enforcement and the judicial process in this country. In fact, he was one of the first investors to contribute to the project to which the three of us are currently consigned. As a result, he is somewhat familiar with what I do, and subsequently, what...*the two of you* do for me."

Jacob hit the elevator button. "Does he know we're coming?"

"I'll place a call. He'll be expecting your visit." A moment passed. "Mr. St. Christopher, Ms. Stockwell, thank you and...Godspeed."

The elevator doors opened and Jacob and Stockwell stepped into the car. He gave his boss a warm smile. "Try not to worry, Higs." The doors moved. "We'll bring them back."

Mustering a weak smile, Higs watched the doors shut. "From your lips," he whispered, "to God's ears."

. . .

In the first floor garage, Jacob slammed the driver's door of his vintage 1970 Mustang. After tossing his leather jacket into the bright red Ford F-150 that sported matte black rims and black trim, he followed Stockwell to the truck's passenger side. He opened her door before opening the back door, in the opposite direction. "I need to show you something." He lifted the bench seat, revealing a black metal box running the full width of the backseat. "I had this installed yesterday." He pointed at a control panel. "Put your finger here."

She touched the scanner.

"Now punch in the four-digit security code...month and day of our first date."

Her jaw slackening, she slowly turned her head toward him.

He gaped at her blank stare. "Seriously? I showed up at your place...with pizza in hand?"

"We said that wasn't really a date."

"Please, Stockwell. We both know that was a date."

"Okay fine. It was a date." She smiled to herself, recalling the evening. *And a nice one at that.* A beat. "So..." she eyed the numbers on the panel and wiggled her fingers, "was that a Tuesday or a Wednesday night?"

Smiling, he glanced down for a moment and slid fingers into the front pockets of his blue jeans. "You don't remember, do you? I thought women were supposed to be good with these...*special firsts*; first date, first kiss, first six-and-a-half-week anniversary."

"Of course I remember. It was just last month." Stockwell tapped 'zero' and 'six' before twirling a finger in the air and hitting two numbers. The line of dots on the panel blinked red. She paired two other numbers with the 'zero' and the 'six.' The dots blinked red.

"Just so you know; you're locked out after three tries."

Facing him, she put a hand on his chest, on his medium gray, banded-collar dress shirt. "I know you're having fun with this, but," she paused, "the code?"

He snickered. "Zero-six-two-zero."

"That was my next try." She keyed in the numbers and the internal locks released.

Shaking his head, Jacob lifted the lid. Inside the steel box: weapons, loaded magazines, boxes of ammunition, clothing, boots and specialty gear.

"What is it with you and the..." her mind envisioning a similar cache in the trunk of his Mustang, she flipped over a hand at the tactical display in front of her, "secret stashes of guns and ammo?"

"Occupational necessity." He gestured. "You have the left side. My stuff's on the right."

Fumbling around inside her half of the storage compartment, she moved a few items, lifted a cardboard box and faced him. "I see you've thought of everything."

He eyed the tampons. "I've got your back covered, Stockwell." He dithered. "Although in this case, it seems more like I'm covering your..."

She raised an eyebrow at her man.

Feeling his cheeks getting warm, he replaced the feminine hygiene product, cleared his throat and shut the lid on the metal box. "Just don't tell Higs about the *secret stash.* I'm waiting for the right time to explain this latest...five-figure line item on the financial statement."

Regarding the side of his darkening face, she inwardly sniggered. *I so love it when you blush.*

Jacob pointed toward the other end. "There's another keypad down there; both will accept any of your fingerprints. And the code is—"

"Wait a minute." Stockwell confronted him. "How'd you get my fingerprints?"

"I lifted them from some of the *many glasses* you leave around the house...on a daily basis." A moment passed. "How do you go through so many—" he waved a hand, "never mind. It's not important. I love having you around." He motioned toward the keypads. "The code's the same for both."

She nodded. "Got it," a beat, "and I'll cut down on my drinking glasses."

"Don't worry about it...really. I've lived by myself for three years now and I'm just not accustomed to seeing things around the house that I didn't put there. I'll get used to it. Forget I said anything." After closing the back door, "We should go," he took her hand and helped her into the F-150.

She placed a black, two-inch, chunky-heeled shoe on the running board. "Thank you."

He ogled bare legs below her violet, tulip-style skirt with a matching three-quarter sleeve jacket. The skirt's hem hugged her thighs.

"I saw that, Mr. St. Christopher."

Flashing a grin, "Can't help myself," he shut the door.

Minutes later, Jacob and Stockwell were heading for I-278. Behind them, the Keep's steel bollards were rising from the concrete in front of the slowly closing, reinforced steel roll-up door. One hand on the steering wheel, he put his free elbow on the center console and lowered his forearm toward her.

She took his hand.

He squeezed lightly. "Dear God, protect us as we carry out this mission. Give us the wisdom to find Ayda and Zoe, and the strength to bring them home to their loved ones. In Jesus' name, we pray. Amen."

Rolling onto her left hip and crossing her legs, Stockwell kissed the back of his hand. "Amen."

11:27 A.M.
WAPPINGERS FALLS
DUTCHESS COUNTY, NEW YORK

Jacob stopped the Ford F-150 at the end of a court and shut off the engine. He noted one black SUV parked on the street and another in the driveway on his two o'clock, the driveway of Paul and Lisa Gentry. Both vehicles had government plates. He surveyed the neighborhood.

The homes in this subdivision were virtually the same; two-story with narrow and deep lots; shrubs around the base of the house; small trees that topped out below the roofline; well-manicured front lawns to the side of a double-wide driveway.

Jacob came back to the Gentry's home. Their lot sloped away from the structure and up to a small creek in the distance. They were the only homeowners to have a large tree in their backyard, an oak that rose twice as high as the house. He eyed Stockwell. "You want to take point on this?"

Opening her door, she gave him a sharp nod. "I can do that."

He climbed down from the truck, slipped arms into his leather jacket, concealing the Coonan under his left armpit, and met her at the front bumper. The two strolled up the driveway, making it as far as a black Mercedes, backed up to the garage, before hearing a voice.

"Jacob St. Christopher. Do my eyes deceive me?"

Jacob and Stockwell turned around and watched a man, in a black suit and tie, follow the same path they had taken.

"How the heck are you?" The man held out a hand.

Seeing his reflection in mirrored sunglasses, Jacob shook the offering. "Carter."

The black man in his mid-thirties stood a couple inches shorter than Jacob did and sported a goatee and closely cropped hair. Carter removed his eyewear, stowed them in an inside jacket pocket and nodded at Stockwell. "Agent Stockwell."

"Agent Williams."

He eyed Jacob. "What have you been doing for the last three years? No one's seen or heard from you."

Jacob glimpsed Stockwell and half shrugged at Carter. "I've been around." The two men had a short stint on the FBI's SWAT team, until Carter returned to the field after the birth of his son.

"How've you been, since what happened to—"

"I'm getting by. And you? How's little Timothy? He must be four or five by now, right?"

Carter hesitated, glanced at Stockwell and came back to Jacob. "Tim's...Tim's going to be five next month. He's a handful...keeps Maggie running. That's for sure."

Jacob smiled.

"She'll be glad when he starts school this fall. She tells me all the time she's looking forward to her...*vacation.*"

"I'll bet she is." Jacob pivoted his upper body toward the house before squaring his frame with the male FBI agent.

"So are the rumors true, Jake? Are you working for Homeland Security these days?"

"They are. I am."

"That's great. Glad to see you're still in the game." Carter's attention moved back and forth from Jacob to Stockwell before his gaze settled on the latter. "So why are you here, Stockwell?"

She jerked a thumb over her shoulder. "We're here to speak with the Gentry's...about their missing daughters."

"The agency's assigned the case to me."

She pumped her hands toward Carter. "And it's still yours. Mr. Gentry has asked to speak with us. That's all."

The man furled his brow. "Why?"

"I can't say."

After several long moments of scrutinizing his law enforcement counterparts, Carter squinted at Jacob and Stockwell. "Since when is Homeland in bed with the FBI anyway?"

"We're not." Jacob studied the asphalt. "We're taking this new venture slowly, getting to know each other first, getting to know each other's moves."

Stockwell shot a sideways look at her partner.

"If all goes well," Jacob sent a half smile toward Carter that was meant for her, "*then...we'll be sleeping with each other.*"

Stockwell crossed her arms over her chest, shifted weight to one foot and stared at Jacob.

Carter flicked his eyes back and forth between the two agents. "Okay...well..." he scratched his chin, "*whatever's* going on here...I'll introduce you to the Gentry's." Carter took a step. "Follow me."

"If you don't mind," Jacob raised a hand, "we'll take it from here. Mr. and Mrs. Gentry are expecting us."

Carter bobbed his eyebrows and gave the front door a quick scan. "If you say so." He smacked the taller man's shoulder. "Don't be a stranger. It was good seeing you."

Jacob nodded. "You too. Give my best to Maggie."

"I will." Carter glimpsed Stockwell, "Agent Stockwell."

She broke off the death stare with her man and acknowledged her fellow agent. "Williams."

Carter strode down the driveway.

Jacob took the short 'L-shaped' sidewalk to the front door and pressed the doorbell.

Stockwell stood next to him and resumed her earlier posture, arms crossed, weight to one side.

Doing his best to hide his amusement, but failing, Jacob eyed the rubber doormat—black with 'WELCOME' embossed in the center. "Whatever you're going to say or do, you should do so now." He motioned. "That door's going to open. And you'll have lost your window of opportunity."

"You're toying with me, Mr. St. Christopher."

He grinned.

"Just remember, I can toy and tease as well." A beat. "And now that we're sharing a living space, I have some pretty skimpy clothes I can wear from my bedroom to the bathroom...or while cooking breakfast, or watching TV with you."

"You're sending mixed signals, Stockwell. Is that supposed to frighten or *excite* me?"

"You tell me. Since we're," she put a finger to her lips, "how'd you put that to Agent Williams? Oh yeah...since we're *taking this new venture slowly*, you won't be able to act on any," she paused, "impulses you may have."

Jacob's face went deadpan before he pursed his lips and barely nodded. "Well played, Miss Stockwell."

"I believe that's called...check and mate."

He snickered. "*Very* well played."

The door opened. At five-nine and in his early fifties, a man wearing black slacks and a blue, eggshell-colored dress shirt stood in the doorway. His dark blue tie stopped at the beginnings of a beer belly. "Can I help you?"

Jacob eyed the man. "Mr. Gentry?"

"Yes?" Wide, dark brown eyeglasses magnified Gentry's unstable eyes.

"I'm St. Christopher." Jacob motioned. "This is Agent Stockwell. Alfred—"

"Oh yes of course." Gentry stepped backward. "Please come in."

The agents entered the home.

After shaking hands with his guests, "My wife's in the reading room," he led them to the far side of the house and into a cozy, well-lit space. Opposite the door, a big bay window provided plenty of reading light during the day. On the left and right walls were seven-foot-high shelves, filled with books. A couch lay a few feet in front of each bookcase. Each sofa faced the other. Two easy chairs rested near the window; on either side of the entry door sat another. Floor lamps were strategically placed for reading at night.

Dressed in a dark, knee-length skirt, white blouse, tan nylons and black flats, Mrs. Gentry stood near the window, her back to the door. Hunched over, her head down, her auburn, collar-length hair covering her ears, the woman sniffed.

"Lisa honey?"

She half turned her upper body.

"The people I told you were coming..."

Her arms folded, she held her head in one hand. Spotting the visitors, she righted herself, swiped fingers over her cheeks and straightened her shirt.

"...they're here."

Gentry met his wife at the window, put an arm around her waist and led her to the middle of the room, stopping between the couches. "This is," he paused, "I'm sorry. I didn't get your first names."

Jacob drew nearer to the grieving mother and took her hand in both of his. "I'm Jacob St. Christopher. I'm very sorry about what happened to your daughters, ma'am."

Stockwell approached.

He gestured. "This is my partner, Special Agent Deanna Stockwell."

Stockwell gave the woman a disappearing smile. "Pleased to meet you, Mrs. Gentry. I wish it were under better circumstances."

"Thank you. And please call me Lisa."

Jacob and Stockwell: "Thank you."

Gentry gestured toward one couch, "Please," while he and his wife sat in the other. He leaned back and crossed his legs, while Lisa sat erect, knees pressed together, hands folded on her lap.

The agents mimicked the woman's posture, sitting upright. "I realize," Stockwell crossed her legs and rested interlaced fingers on her knees, "you've already been through the details of that night with police and the FBI, but would you mind going over it again with us?"

"Certainly." Lisa lowered her chin to her chest and took a breath.

Gentry uncrossed his legs, rocked forward and laid a hand on hers. "Let me, hon." He eyed Jacob and Stockwell. "Ayda and Zoe left around seven that night. They were to pick up their friend—Belle—at her house before going out...to celebrate Belle's upcoming wedding." Gentry dipped his head toward his wife. "We were home all night. We went to bed around eleven-thirty. I sent Ayda a quick text message, making sure the girls were okay. Fifteen or twenty minutes later, I got a reply. It was short and written in," he shook his head, "that shortened code kids use today...acronyms, a bunch of missing letters...you know what I mean."

Stockwell smiled and nodded.

"Anyway, I knew they were fine, so I went to sleep. Hours later, the next thing I hear is the doorbell ringing. The police are on our doorstep, telling me they think our daughters were taken."

Lisa put a hand over her mouth.

He wrapped his left arm around her shoulders. "The

FBI got involved and now," he lifted an upturned palm and shrugged, "and now we're waiting for them to find our kids."

"Was there," Stockwell observed Gentry, "anything unusual about the text from Ayda?"

He looked away before slowly shaking his head. "No. It was typical Ayda—short and to the point." His phone rang. He dug out the device and glimpsed the screen.

Jacob squinted at the man.

His face losing color, "I'm sorry," Gentry stood, "but I have to take this."

"Paul," Lisa looked up at her husband, "they're here to help us." She flicked her eyes toward the cell and scowled. "Can't it wait?"

"It'll only take a second." He kissed her cheek and darted into a room off the main space and half closed the adjoining door.

She huffed and came back to the agents. "I'm sorry. It's probably something to do with this stupid dinner party tonight."

Stockwell glanced at Jacob.

He frowned at her.

She turned back to Lisa. "Dinner party?"

"It's for investors. My husband owns a security software company and he's meeting with investors to ask for another round of," she made a face, "of...capital..." before shaking her head, "money. He's asking them for more money."

Rising from his seat, Jacob meandered over to the bookcase behind Lisa. Standing near the door to the partially open adjoining door, he slid a book off the shelf and thumbed the pages. Over his shoulder, Stockwell continued the questioning.

"We understand a ransom demand was made."

"Yes. My husband got a text message a few hours ago...around eight o'clock I think."

Stockwell nodded, knowing the FBI had not been able to track the number.

"The FBI man said it was untraceable."

Out of the corner of her eye, Stockwell watched Jacob replace a book and select another.

"Anyway, Paul's in the process of getting the money ready...for the drop-off tonight."

"At ten o'clock." Stockwell glimpsed Jacob again. *What's the heck's he doing over there?*

"Yes. That's right."

Coming back to Lisa, "Did the kidnappers," Stockwell saw Jacob in her peripheral vision, shelving the book and backing away from the case, "leave any specific instructions, regarding the meet tonight?"

Gentry hurried into the room, looking down and glowering at his cell.

The two men bumped into each other.

Gentry's mobile fell to the floor.

Jacob stooped. "Please forgive me, sir."

"That's all right."

Jacob glanced at the screen, while handing over the device. "I was just admiring your collection of books. You're quite the scholarly man, Mr. Gentry."

He stowed his phone and regarded the shelves. "Yes, well...it pays to stay up on things. An active mind is a strong mind."

"I couldn't agree with you more. I love to read."

Stockwell puckered her brow at Jacob. *I've yet to see a book anywhere in your house.*

Gentry leaned away a little. "Oh really? What do you read?"

"Mostly sports magazines, the comics, the backs of cereal boxes."

Gentry wrinkled his forehead.

Jacob chuckled. "I'm kidding, sir. In stressful situations like this, I find a little humor can be helpful. And," he pointed at the pants pocket where the man had slid the phone, "that call looked pretty serious. Is everything okay?"

Gentry looked down at the rectangle outline on his pants. "Oh...yeah...that, that was just some last-minute details on another matter." He led Jacob back to the couches.

"The party tonight?"

Gentry sat next to his wife and lifted his chin toward his male counterpart. "Pardon me?"

Sitting, Jacob motioned toward Lisa. "Your wife told us you're hosting a party for investors tonight. I imagine you'd want to get everything just perfect for something like that."

The older man blinked several times, glimpsed his wife and looked at Jacob. "Right...yes, it was just an issue with the restaurant. It was nothing."

"Paul, you're not honestly thinking of still going to that, are you?"

"Honey, I only have to make an appearance."

"Paul, for—"

"I'll only be gone an hour. I promise. It's important I show up."

Lisa scooted away and squared shoulders with her mate. "Our daughters are God knows where right now, being held at gunpoint for all we know, and you want to go socialize?"

"Honey, I—"

"Ayda doesn't even have her inhaler with her. You know how she gets when she's stressed."

Jacob shot a look toward Stockwell, who produced her phone and opened the case files Higs had sent.

"Paul, she needs that medication or she could die."

"Excuse me." Jacob lifted a hand toward Lisa. "What does Ayda use an inhaler for?"

Gentry faced his questioner. "She's had asthma her whole life. Fortunately, she's been able to keep it under control, but when she gets excited, it can flare up."

"And," Lisa raised her voice, "it can *kill her*, Paul."

He reached for his wife. "It's going to be okay. She's

going to—"

Lisa swatted at his hands and stormed over to the window.

Jacob rose to his feet.

Stockwell joined him and motioned toward her cell. "It's in Higs' notes," she whispered. "Ayda has asthma and..."

Hearing the hesitation in her speech pattern, he spied his teammate and saw a look that matched her faltering voice.

"...her inhaler was found at the crime scene."

He gritted his teeth at the implication.

"Wherever she is, Jake, she doesn't have her medicine."

Gentry stood and glimpsed his guests. "I'm sorry. My wife can get a little," he paused before lowering his voice, "*emotional* in a crisis. If you don't mind, I think it best I walk you out now."

Stockwell forced a smile. "We understand." She followed the host to the door.

Jacob walked the other way, drawing up behind Lisa. "Ma'am?"

She turned around.

He peered into glossy eyes. "In circumstances like these, most people would say...I know what you're going through." A beat. "But most of them wouldn't have a clue."

The woman caught a tear, as it raced down her cheek.

Jacob forfeited his handkerchief.

She accepted the folded cotton square. "Thank you."

He took a forward step and gently held her upper arms. "I, on the other hand, know *exactly* what you're experiencing." A moment passed. "Three years ago, my daughter was taken. She's still missing."

Her lips parting, Lisa gaped at him. "I'm so sorry."

"Thank you."

"What happened?"

"She left for school one morning and sh—" his chest swelling, Jacob faltered.

Lisa cupped one of his elbows.

"She never came home."

"That's awful. How old was she?"

"Thirteen." Jacob blinked a few times and swallowed. "What I'm trying to tell you is, *to me*...your daughters are not just another missing person's case." Staring at the woman, he saw the same expression he had seen in his ex-wife's eyes when he told her their daughter had been abducted. "I promise you. I'm going to do everything in my power to find Ayda and Zoe. You just have to have a little faith, ma'am."

Lisa sniffed, brushed the cotton article across her nose and ogled him for several moments. "I believe you. Thank you, Mr. St. Christopher."

He gave her a warm smile. "Call me Jacob."

She smiled back before drying her eyes. "Thank you...Jacob."

He lightly squeezed her arms and strode toward a waiting Stockwell and Paul Gentry.

Jacob and Stockwell stepped onto the front porch. She pivoted toward Gentry. "Thank you for your time, Mr. Gentry. We appreciate you meeting with us. If you think of anything that might be useful," she held out a business card, "please call this number. It's a direct line to my cell phone."

He took the card. "Thank you. I will."

"Mr. Gentry," his arms crossed over his chest, Jacob confronted the elder man, "can you think of anyone who might want to get to you...through your family? Do you have any enemies? Has anyone made any threats against you?"

Expanding his lungs, while hoisting his pants, Gentry looked away. He blew out the air and came back to Jacob. "I can't think of anyone. The industry I'm in is competitive, but I can't see someone doing this sort of thing to get back at me."

Jacob squinted at the man for a few, intense moments.

Gentry flicked his eyes back and forth from Stockwell to Jacob a couple times.

"All right then." Jacob shook the man's hand. "Thank you for your time. We'll be in touch if we find something."

"Thank you—both of you—for doing what you can."

Stockwell smiled. "You're welcome." She pointed at the card he held. "Call me if you remember anything."

"I will."

Jacob and Stockwell walked down the driveway, climbed into the F-150 and slammed doors. Putting his elbow on the door and gazing out his window, he stroked his chin. After attaching her seatbelt and situating the shoulder harness, she spied him. "I saw what you did in there."

He faced her.

"You took a step toward Mr. Gentry when he entered the room. You were smooth, but I know you collided with him on purpose. Why'd you do that?"

"I wanted to see who called him."

She hiked her eyebrows. "And?"

"The number was blocked."

"Why?"

He shrugged. "Why does anybody block their number?"

"That's," she briefly shut her eyes, "not what I meant. Why did you want to know who called him?"

Shifting in his seat, Jacob aimed his torso at her. "What's your assessment of Mr. Gentry?"

She rotated palms upward and half turned away. "He's a man under stress...over his daughters being kidnapped. Plus, he seems to be pulled in different directions; his wife, his kids, his job." She squinted at her man. "Where's this going, Jake?"

Jacob massaged his forehead before washing the hand down his face. "It's been two days, since Ayda and Zoe's disappearance." A beat. "Two days after D.D. went missing, I—" his chest heaved, "well...let's just say I couldn't function very well. I certainly wasn't in the frame of mind to attend dinner parties and sweet-talk investors."

Stockwell leaned away from him. "Jake, are you thinking that Mr. Gentry..."

"I don't know what I'm thinking at this point. All I'm doing is pointing out the facts as I see them." He extended a hand toward the passenger, palm up. "And how can someone act so cool, knowing his daughter could die without her inhaler? I would be beside myself, doing everything I could to find the S.O.B.'s that took her." He paused. "I *was* beside myself. I *did* do everything I could to..." he turned away and huffed. "Actually...maybe I *didn't* do everything in my power to find her. Or maybe," he wavered, while squeezing the steering wheel tighter, "or maybe she'd still be—"

"Stop it, Jake. Just knock it off." She loosened his grip on the wheel and held his hand. "I may not have been with you then, but I am now, *right here and now*. And I know what kind of man you are. I know that you would've given everything to find your daughter. So stop that kind of talk right now. You hear me?"

Silence consumed the interior for the better part of a minute.

With his free hand, Jacob retrieved his cell phone and tapped the screen a few times.

"Who are you calling?"

"Higs."

Stockwell rotated her head and peered at him out of one, half-open eye. "Why?"

"I want him to do some digging...on Gentry."

"Jake, you can't do that. You heard Higs this morning. The two of them are good friends. You can't ask Higs to spy on his friend."

"I'm not asking him to—" Jacob faced the windshield. "Higs, it's me. I need you to find out everything you can on..."

Stockwell put a death grip on his hand and nearly climbed over the center console. She whipped her head back and forth, while mouthing the word 'No' several times.

He pumped a hand her way. "...on your friend, Paul Gentry. There might be something in his past that can lead us to who kidnapped his kids. He's under a lot of duress. People in those situations can't always remember details; details that could help solve cases." Jacob arched his eyebrows at Stockwell and mimed, 'Happy now?'

She relaxed a bit and returned to her seat.

"Thanks Higs. Get back to me if you find something. Stockwell and I are going to check out the crime scene. We'll call if we uncover anything." He tapped the 'end' icon and observed his woman. "There...I didn't say anything about my theory."

"And let's just hope it stays that way...a theory."

Jacob started the Ford and navigated the four-by-four out of the court. A mile down the road, he glimpsed Stockwell before watching the traffic again. "Thanks."

She had her phone out, giving the information from Higs a second go-through. "For?"

"For talking me down from the ledge..."

She turned toward him.

"...about D.D."

She smiled. "That's why I'm here. Well, that's *one* of the reasons anyway...support."

Jacob watched another mile of landscape go by the truck.

Stockwell kept her nose in her phone.

"You'd have liked her."

She faced him.

"I wish you could've met her. You'd have liked her."

"I know I will. One day...*when we find her*...you can introduce me properly."

Hearing her speak in the future tense, he lifted one side of his mouth.

"And we'll have a good time, doing our nails, getting our hair done, talking about boys."

Jacob's finger shot upward. "That's a big fat 'No' on the last one." He wagged the finger. "No boys."

She snickered. "You won't be able to keep her from falling in love, Jake. You..."

"Like hell I can't."

"...can only," another chuckle from Stockwell, as she took his hand, "you can only show her how a good man is supposed to treat a woman. And in my book, you're terrific at that."

He half grinned.

She returned to staring at the information on her mobile.

Two miles later, Jacob kissed the back of her hand before lowering his forearm to the console.

Spying him in her peripheral vision, feeling her heart beating faster, she gripped his hand a little tighter.

12:17 P.M.

Five-six, athletic build; long, straight and wispy, strawberry blonde hair; blue eyes; narrow nose and a full lower lip, Ayda and Zoe looked the same. At this moment, however, it was easy to distinguish one from the other.

Curled up into a ball on the floor, wheezing and coughing, Ayda hugged herself. Her head was full and pressure was building. Her lower jaw moving up and down, she cycled through the motions to get a breath. Only tiny gasps of air came.

Zoe swiped at the clown mask, her fingernails finding soft flesh.

The kidnapper's head whipped to his right before he pinned the woman against the brick wall with his left arm. He ran the back of his free hand over his temple and gaped at the blood on the first two knuckles.

"She's dying. Give it to me."

Clown 1 pivoted his head toward the moaning woman in a fetal position before coming back to Zoe. He held up an object.

Zoe reached.

Clown 1 pulled the inhaler back a hair.

Her fingers closed around nothing.

He laughed.

"Give it to me," she screamed, "or I swear I'll kill you myself."

He laughed again, removed his forearm from her chest, tossed the medication into the air and walked away.

In one motion, Zoe caught the plastic tube, dropped to her knees, hefted her sister into a sitting position and administered the drug. She clutched Ayda's hands and held her attention. "Look at me, Ay." She sat on her ankles and got closer to Ayda. "Look at me. Focus...focus on getting that first breath."

Against the wall, Ayda rocked backward, as her chest curved outward.

Zoe cupped the back of her older sister's head to keep her from hitting the wall. "Just get that first one." Over her shoulder, she heard laughing. She shook the inhaler, pushed it into Ayda's mouth and gave her another dose. "Come on, Ay. Just give me one."

Ayda sat straight and filled her lungs for the first time in nearly two minutes.

"That's it. Everything's going to be just fine." Holding Ayda's head in both hands and locking eyes with her twin, "Can you," Zoe took an exaggerated breath, "give me another one?"

Ayda took a second breath. The tightness in her chest dissipated.

"That a girl." Zoe sat and cradled her sister.

Ayda took her third breath. The throbbing in her temple slowed. Hugging her abdomen, she laid her head on Zoe's chest.

Still chuckling, the two Clowns left the room.

Zoe watched the door slam shut. A second later, she heard a key move a deadbolt. The barren, chilly, darkened room was lit by a small, obscured window near the low ceiling to her right. The concrete floor was cold on her butt. She and Ayda only had the clothes they wore to the party—tight skirts, blouses and high heels.

Five minutes passed.

Ayda stirred. "You," she coughed, "you shouldn't have done that."

Zoe peeked at the top of her relative's hair.

"They could have killed you."

Zoe gripped Ayda a little tighter. "How are you feeling?"

"Better—" Ayda shivered, "thank you."

Zoe unbuttoned and slipped off her shirt before covering her sister with the garment.

"No, it's freezing down here. You'll—"

"Oh shut up, will you? You're in no condition to fight me anyway." With only a black bra covering her upper body, the younger sibling resumed her hold on Ayda, gritted her teeth and slowly pressed her bare back to the cold cinder block.

Minutes elapsed.

Ayda lifted her eyes and glimpsed the bottom of Zoe's chin. "Hey Zo Zo?"

"Yeah?" A few seconds went by. "What is it, Ay?"

"I'm sorry for what I said about you...when we were in the alley. I—I didn't mean anything by it."

"I know." Zoe half grinned. "It's not your fault you got an extra helping of the 'mom gene.'"

Ayda snickered. "Sounds like you've had that one in the holster for some time."

"No, I just came up with it." Stillness surrounded them. Zoe hated the quiet. She always had to have something going—music, the television, a humming fan, anything, but absolute silence. "I'm sorry too...for telling you to bite me."

"Don't worr—"

"If it's any consolation, I had a lot more, *worse* names running through my head at the time."

Ayda laughed.

"Hey, do you remember that time in high school we stole Dad's car and made a night of it?"

Ayda huffed. "You mean *you* stole Dad's car and took me hostage."

Zoe lifted a shoulder. "Six of one...half dozen of another."

"What made you think of that?"

Zoe looked around and dipped her forehead toward nothing in particular. "This...being kidnapped."

Ayda nodded. "Ah...like how you kidnapped *me*?"

"Okay fine. I kidnapped you and took you on an adventure. Now don't tell me you didn't have a blast." Silence. "Yeah, that's what I thought. That's the first time I remember you ever digging your panties out of your crack and really having fun."

Ayda chuckled. "Thanks for the image."

"So you never told me. What happened between you and Tony Woje...Woje-dub...Woje..."

"Wojedubokowski?"

Zoe nodded. "Sure. What happened between you two that night? You disappeared for almost an hour. Did you...you know...*do* something...*together*?"

A broad grin washed over Ayda's face.

Staring at the wooden beams overhead, Zoe felt the change in her sister's demeanor. She smiled at the splintered planks. "You little tramp you."

Ayda slapped Zoe's leg.

Zoe giggled. "So are you going to tell me?"

"Tell you what?"

The younger woman rolled her eyes. "Oh please. Tony. How was Tony?"

"It's not only gentlemen; ladies don't kiss and tell either."

"And...they're back up there again."

Ayda frowned. "What?"

"Your underwear; they just got wedged up your butt again."

Sniggering, Ayda brought her knees closer to her

chest and curled her hand under her chin. Her mind drifted back to the incident with the stolen car, and Tony. She smiled. After another moment of reflection, she whispered, "It was great."

Her head resting against the wall, her eyes closed, Zoe beamed. "What happened to ladies don't tell?"

"It doesn't count between sisters."

Thirty seconds later, the smile returned to Zoe's face. "So was his last name the only *long* thing about him?"

Ayda's eyes grew wide and she pinched her sister's inner thigh, near the knee.

Zoe yelped, rubbed the tender spot and laughed before draping the makeshift blanket over Ayda again.

After another ten minutes of Zoe jabbering to fill the void, she stood, covered Ayda with the shirt and wandered toward the faint beam of light.

"What are you doing?"

Staring at the tiny window, Zoe rubbed the backs of her upper arms. "I think I could squeeze through there."

Ayda lifted her gaze toward the window. "You're too big."

Zoe whipped her head toward the older Gentry. "Hey I've been working out." Coming back to the elevated exit point, "I'd even bet..." she lifted arms over her head; the lower part of the sill touched her wrists, "I weigh less than you do."

Ayda snorted. "We're identical twins, Zo Zo. Even a few pounds lighter than me, you're not fitting through that window."

"Not with that kind of an attitude I won't."

"Besides, we have no idea where we are. We could be in the middle of a forest for all we know."

"No," Zoe stepped back and removed her spike-heeled shoe, her focus going back and forth from the footwear to the glass, "we weren't in the van that long. I'm guessing we're still in the city...possibly just on the outskirts." After a second back-and-forth, she spied Ayda. "You feel up to giving me a boost?"

CHAPTER 9
MINIVAN

2:39 P.M.
NEW YORK CITY

For the last thirty minutes, Jacob and Stockwell had been canvassing the parking lot, where the kidnapping took place. While en route from the Gentry's home, she had obtained digital photos from the FBI agents first at the scene. The pictures showed Ayda's vehicle; the vehicle's interior, from several angles, and the woman's discarded purse on the pavement, near the left rear tire.

Jacob stood in the center of three painted lines, the space in which Ayda's car had been parked. Arms folded across his chest, the fingertips of one hand stroking his chin, he did a slow, three-sixty pivot.

Having learned this was his process, getting in the mind of the victim, and the perpetrator, and seeing the surroundings from their perspective, Stockwell left him alone. Leaning back against the F-150's front grille, the heel of one shoe hooked on the bumper, she flipped through photos on her cell phone.

Jacob made another turn, stopping at the three-quarter mark. "Hey Stockwell...bring your phone over here."

She pushed off from the truck and joined him. "What's up?"

"Where was Ayda's purse found again?"

She ran a forefinger across the mobile's screen several times and took a few steps forward. "Right about here."

Jacob slid left, stood in front of her and squinted at something in the distance.

Standing on his left, she glimpsed his sulking face. "What is it?"

"Did the temperature dip down last night in New York City?"

"Not just in the city. I had to grab an extra blanket in the middle of the night myself. Why?"

Jacob jutted out his chin at a black man getting out of the sliding door on an older model minivan; a blanket was wrapped around his body. "Today warmed up pretty quickly though."

She eyed the man near the open side door; he took off the covering, folded the fabric into a smaller square and returned it to the van. She barely shook her head. "It certainly isn't blanket weather *now*."

"No, it's not." Jacob made a beeline for the man, his partner by his side. "Excuse me, sir?"

Wearing a white t-shirt, blue jeans and stocking feet, the man glanced over his shoulder, slammed the side panel and opened the driver door.

Jacob increased his pace to a jog. He grabbed the closing door. "Excuse me, sir. I need to talk to you."

"Well, I don't need to talk to you." T-shirt pulled. Jacob held firm.

"Yes," Stockwell flashed her badge, "you do...FBI."

Grimacing, the man let go of the door. "Look, I didn't do anything. I was just taking a nap. I don't want any trouble."

Moving to the sliding door, "Who said you were in trouble?" Jacob pressed his nose to the window and put cupped hands to his temples; two eyes stared back at him through the tinted glass. He stood erect.

Peeling out of his seat, "Hey get away from there," the driver advanced toward Jacob.

Jacob sent out a stiff arm and looked up at the man, who was three inches taller and fifty pounds heavier than he was. He drew his 1911 and held the weapon at a forty-five degree angle between him and the muscle-bound brute. "Back it up."

Stockwell drew her firearm and slid left to get a clear shot without endangering Jacob.

"Who's that in the vehicle, sir?"

"It's no one."

Jacob shook his head. "Not good enough. Turn around."

"It's no one. I haven't done anything."

Jacob brought his gun to ninety-degrees. "Turn around...and put your hands on your head."

The man winced and rolled his head before his shoulders slouched. A moment later, he complied.

"Down on your knees."

He knelt.

"Stockwell?"

"I got him." With her Glock pointed at the suspect, she jerked her head toward the vehicle. "Go."

Jacob slid open the side door; a black boy around ten years old, wearing sweatpants and a sweatshirt, was hiding in the cargo area. Jacob glanced around the interior and saw jugs of drinking water, piles of clothing, blankets, food wrappers, shoes, socks and miscellaneous household items. He hid the 357 Magnum from the boy's sight and pumped his free hand. "It's all right, son. We're police. Are you okay?"

The boy's eyes focused on T-shirt. "What's going on, Dad?"

Jacob faced the kneeling man. "This is your son?"

T-shirt hung his head. "Everything's fine, Samuel. You can talk to them."

. . .

2:47 P.M.

Having holstered their guns, Jacob and Stockwell separated; she stayed near the van with Samuel, while he stepped away with T-shirt. Jacob held out a driver's license. "So Morgan...you've been living in a minivan with your son? For how long?"

Morgan claimed his ID. "Since I lost my house." He slipped the card into a brown wallet.

"That doesn't answer my question."

"Look, you've fulfilled your duty to investigate a potential crime," he waved a dismissive hand, "satisfied your probable cause...whatever. Nothing's going on here. Can we leave now?"

"I just have a few questions for you."

Morgan put his hands on his hips and looked away.

"Do you park your van here often...overnight I mean?"

The big man was silent.

"This will go a lot smoother if you answer my questions."

After several moments, Morgan came back to his interrogator. "We stay in different places."

"Were you parked here a few days ago, on the night of the twenty-first?"

"I...I don't remember."

"Did you see the three girls, the ones who were attacked?"

Morgan flicked his eyes toward the area beyond Jacob's shoulder and quickly came back to him. "Nope."

Jacob squinted at the man. "Are you sure?"

"Positive. Can I take my son and go now?"

After glancing at Stockwell, who was sitting on her haunches, playing a game with the ten-year-old, Jacob regarded the boy's father. "You hungry?"

Morgan's eyebrows came together.

"I haven't eaten anything in..." Jacob spied his watch, "well it's going on eight hours now. I'm starving. How about we grab a bite to eat? My treat."

After scrutinizing the federal agent, Morgan lifted a hand. "Look, I see what you're doing, but I'm not accustomed to taking charity. Are we done here?"

Jacob aimed a finger at Samuel. "What about your son?"

"What about him?"

"When was the last time he ate...ate until his belly was stuffed?"

"I told you—"

"You don't take charity. I know. I get it. I'm a proud man too." Jacob paused. "But think of your son. He's not old enough to let his pride get in the way of something good."

Morgan cranked his head around, toward his offspring.

"There's a little diner around the corner from here...great burgers. I think they serve breakfast all day long too."

Morgan pivoted back and stared at Jacob.

The agent cocked his head to one side.

Stockwell laughed.

Samuel giggled.

Jacob glimpsed her. "It looks like my partner and your son are getting along pretty well. Maybe he'll even make a new friend in the process."

"I'm sorry. Are you in law enforcement...or sales?"

Jacob chuckled.

"I'll put on some shoes and meet you there."

"I haven't told you the name of the restaurant."

"I'm familiar with the place." Turning his back on Jacob, Morgan waved off the other man. "I've been there a dozen times."

3:33 P.M.

The small diner was almost empty. The late lunch crowd had left, while a few elderly people—newspaper in hand—had meandered in for coffee. A young man was busy going from table to table, clearing dirty dishes and cleaning booths. His coworker, Melissa, holding a large serving tray high, turned her body sideways and slipped by him.

"Okay," Melissa put the tray on the table across the aisle from her patrons, "I have two burgers with fries." She set a plate in front of Jacob and one in front of Stockwell. She picked up another plate and handed it to Morgan. "And pancakes and bacon..." she poked a finger at Samuel, "*crispy bacon...for you.*"

The little boy smiled, "Thank you," while watching the dinnerware come his way.

Melissa smiled back. "You're very welcome." She eyed Morgan. "Are you sure I can't get you anything, sir?"

He waved a hand between the two of them. "I'm fine. Thank you."

"All right then," she surveyed her handiwork, retrieved the tray and gave everyone a bright smile, "if you need anything, just holler. I'll be back in a little bit to check on you.”

Stockwell unfolded her napkin and spread the linen across her lap. “Thank you, Melissa.”

“Yes,” sitting on the end of the booth, on Stockwell’s right, Jacob pushed his plate away from him, “thank you.” After watching Samuel attack the stack of pancakes, which were now drenched in syrup, he focused his attention on the man across from him. “You never said how long you’ve been living in your van.”

Morgan turned away from his son. The man’s face was stoic again.

Jacob grabbed a fry and pointed the floppy potato at the preteen, “You know...my middle name is Samuel,” before taking a bite. “It’s a good name, a strong name. Did your mother give you that name?”

Morgan bristled.

Samuel shook his head. “Mom died.”

Jacob sat erect.

Bringing her burger to her mouth, Stockwell stopped short of taking a bite.

Morgan put his arm around his son’s shoulder. “Listen, little man, you keep eating. I’m going to speak with Mr. St. Christopher,” he jerked his thumb behind him, “over here.” He lifted eyebrows at Stockwell. “Do you mind watching him?”

“Of course not.”

He nodded, “Thank you,” before standing.

Jacob stood and followed Morgan to an isolated

corner of the diner.

Both men sat across from each other at a booth.

"Look," Morgan rested forearms on the edge of the table and wrung his hands, "I don't want my boy to be a part of this. He doesn't need to hear what happened to his mother all over again."

Jacob nodded. "I understand. What *did* happen?"

"Cancer...an aggressive form...she passed away a year after the diagnosis."

"I'm sorry."

Morgan nodded. "Medical bills came in after she died. I lost my job...and soon after, our home. The same old sob story everyone hears all the time." He looked away and came back to Jacob. "The thing is...when it happens to *you*...it's no longer a sob story. It becomes *real.*"

Jacob pursed his lips and regarded the man.

Morgan's chest heaved before he blew out a gust of wind. "I saw it...everything."

Jacob cocked his head.

"I saw those girls get taken the other night."

Jacob sat straight.

"It happened so fast that I wasn't exactly sure what was going on. One was drunk out of her mind, while the other two helped her lean against the car. A second later, two of them were gone and the third just...slid to her butt." Morgan cracked a couple knuckles. "I didn't know what to do. There *was* nothing I could do. The van was gone. I didn't see anyone."

"Did you call the police?"

"No."

Jacob shot forward in his seat. "Why the hell not? You saw the van. You could've given the police a description. Did you get a license plate number?"

Morgan's eyes never strayed from Samuel. "I got a partial."

Jacob clenched his fists. "Are you serious? What kind of person witnesses a crime and doesn't report—" he rotated his upper body and spied the man's son before turning back and squinting at the other male. He relaxed his hands. "Social Services."

Forearms folded on the table, Morgan eyed Jacob.

"You go to the police...they start asking questions...and they find out a ten-year-old is homeless."

Morgan thrust out a finger toward Samuel. "There's no way in hell I'm losing him. That's my son and he's..." Morgan rammed his thumb into his chest, "he's staying with me. No damn agency's going to take him from me."

Jacob gave Samuel another look and faced the boy's father. "I suppose that explains why you weren't very cooperative back at the van."

Morgan flipped over a hand on the table, palm up. "Police, FBI...ABC, XYZ...you're all the same."

"With all due respect, sir, that's where you're wrong. I'm not here to take away your son."

Morgan glimpsed Samuel, stuffing his mouth full of

pancakes, pancakes that Jacob would be buying. "I know that now."

Jacob studied Morgan. "So what can you tell me about what happened the night those women were abducted?"

Morgan shrugged. "I just did."

"Do you remember any details about the van...see any of the kidnapper's faces? You said you got a partial plate number. What was it?"

"The last three numbers...four-one-two. I saw two men jump out of the van; both were wearing clown masks. They grabbed the women and were gone."

Jacob tipped his head to one side, remembering Higs had said the same thing about the kidnappers wearing clown masks.

Morgan wagged a finger in the air. "The rim...I remember seeing one of the back rims. It was one of those custom wheels, but not your ordinary custom wheels. This one was unique. It had a picture on it, engraved into the metal."

Jacob grabbed a pencil and comment card from a plastic holder. "Can you describe it?"

"It was dark red. I think I saw horns and a pitchfork...you know like the devil." He waved a hand. "But that's not important."

"Why not?"

"There's only one body shop in New York that does that kind of high-end specialty work." He took the writing instrument and white card from Jacob, scribbled something and slid both items back across the table. Morgan pointed. "That's the name of the shop. A friend of mine used to work there a few years ago. I remember stopping by one day and seeing some of the cars they were working on." He tapped the card. "It's the same type of stuff I'm sure I saw on that van."

Jacob tucked the three-by-five cardboard into his jacket pocket. "Did you happen to get a look at the van...make, model, how old?"

"It was an older model...a conversion van, dark," Morgan wavered, "I'm not sure on the color."

Jacob rose to his feet. "Thank you. This gives me a place to start."

"You might want to be careful. My friend quit working there, because the place was becoming a hub for...illegal activity. He never gave any specifics though."

"Thanks for the heads-up." Jacob started back toward Stockwell and Samuel, but stopped. He spun around. "I never asked. What kind of work do you do...*did you do*...before losing your job?"

"Computers. I spent a few years in the Army, specializing in that field."

Jacob lifted his eyebrows. "Really."

"After I got out, I landed a good job with a tech company. It wasn't long after that," he paused, "my wife got sick. I had to take time off work to care for her...doctor visits and stuff like that. The company decided to let me go." Morgan dipped his head toward Jacob. "You know the rest from there."

Jacob squinted at the man. "You have a resume?"

Morgan frowned. "Not on me. Why?"

"I know a guy who's good with computers." A moment passed. "How about a cell phone...you have one of those?"

Morgan huffed. "Yeah...a prepaid one. I'm saving my last few minutes, hoping for a lucky break."

"Give me the number."

Morgan rattled off numbers.

Jacob punched the digits into his cell and stowed the device. "Give me your phone."

Morgan forfeited the black piece of technology.

Jacob entered a number, returned the mobile and pointed. "When that number comes up," he removed several bills from his wallet and held out the cash, "*take the call.*"

Spying the money, Morgan leaned away.

Jacob grabbed one of the man's lifted hands and pressed the folded paper into the palm. "Don't think of it as charity. When you're back on your feet, you can help someone else out."

After staring at the twenties for several long seconds, Morgan let his shoulders slump. "Thank you."

"You bet. Now just make sure you have minutes," Jacob motioned, "on that phone. You got it?" He slapped the man's upper arm and marched back to his teammate.

"Stockwell, we have to go."

She looked up at him. "What's going on?"

"I'll explain on the way." He leaned over the table, "Samuel," and engulfed the boy's hand in his, "it was a pleasure to meet you." He laid a fifty-dollar bill on the table and eyed Morgan. "That's for lunch." For the first time since their meeting, he saw a brief smile flash over the man's face.

Morgan nodded. "Thank you...for everything."

Jacob returned the gesture. "My pleasure."

Getting up from the booth, Stockwell waved. "Bye Sam."

The youngster beamed. "Bye Deanna."

When Jacob and Stockwell had left the diner, Samuel pointed at the full plate of food. "Dad, he forgot to eat."

Sitting next to his son, observing Jacob's departing frame through the windows, "No Sam," Morgan slid Jacob's burger and fries closer, "he didn't forget."

Entering the body shop, Jacob and Stockwell were met with the sound of metal clanging off metal, and the intermittent hissing noise of a sprayer, coming from a sectioned-off area on the other side of the garage. To the left, two men were hunched over the engine compartment of an older model sedan, only their legs and hips visible. Straight ahead, on their knees, wearing coveralls and facemasks, two men were engraving the right front wheel of a red van. The smell of paint and grease permeated the air.

Jacob approached the men next to the van. "Excuse me," he shouted.

The tool in his grasp still running, one man yelled, "What?"

Maintaining his louder than normal voice, Jacob leaned forward a little. "Where can I find the owner?"

The man jerked his thumb over his head, toward the rear of the building. "Follow the music." He touched the rotary implement to the rim; sparks flew.

Jacob nodded. "Thank you."

The agents snaked around power cords and hand

tools, ducked under air hoses and slipped between toolboxes. The hip-hop, rap music grew louder. Walking down a short hall, they came to an open office door, Stockwell stuck fingers into her ears. Jacob banged his fist on the steel door.

His back to them, a bald black man, easily six-six and three hundred pounds, wearing dark pants and a blue shirt—sleeves taut—held a clipboard in one hand and a pen in the other. His attention shifted back and forth from a white, dry erase board on the wall to the portable writing surface.

Opening his mouth, Jacob filled his lungs, "Excu—" before glancing right. He stepped in the same direction and yanked a power cord from an outlet. The music stopped.

"Damn it, Feliz. If you're," Six-Six cursed, "with me again, I swear I'm going to kick your—" Six-Six pivoted and stopped writing when he noticed Jacob and Stockwell. His features hardened. "Who are you?" He glimpsed the cord hanging from Jacob's hand. "And just what the," he cursed, "are you doing, messing around with my tunes?"

Jacob draped the black electrical line over a hook on the wall. "Are you the owner of this shop?" Spying a brown nameplate on the desk, he lifted a finger. "Odell is it?"

Making his way around the desk, Six-Six placed the clipboard on the plastic, faux wood surface.

Jacob cranked his head back, as the man drew nearer to him.

"I said," Six-Six stopped two feet from Jacob, "who the," another foul word, "are you?"

Stockwell held up her cred pack.

He studied the badge.

"And *I said*," Jacob leveled a finger at the man, "are you Odell...and do you own this shop?"

"What the," more swearing, "is this about?"

Shaking his head and looking away, Jacob exhaled a heavy breath. "I'd say you're averaging about five f-bombs a minute." He gestured toward Stockwell. "Let's clean it up for the lady."

Six-Six glared at Stockwell before his eyes dropped to her chest, to her bare legs, "Blondie," before coming back to her breasts again, "doesn't seem bothered by the rough language." He smiled, revealing a gold front tooth. "I'll bet she likes to play rough."

Jacob made fists.

Stockwell took a half step toward her fellow agent and squeezed his nearest forearm. "Okay Odell—are you Odell?" She nodded. "I'm calling you Odell. Odell, it's time you stop wagging your penis and start answering our questions. Because if you keep screwing with us," she lifted a finger, "I can make one phone call, and have a search warrant and an army of agents here," she twirled the digit in the air, "all ready to tear this place from top to bottom. Is that what you want?"

The smirk on the man's face faded.

Holding her hands out at her sides, she gave the office a quick look. "Who knows what we'll find in here...back taxes not paid, out-of-date permits," she locked eyes with him, "hidden records of illegal activities." A beat. "Maybe we'll hit the jackpot and turn up some drugs too."

He clenched his teeth and the muscles at the back of his jaw protruded.

"I guess you're right, Odell." Jacob tipped his head toward his partner. "She does play rough."

The taller man faced Jacob.

"Now...we need to know if you worked on an older model, dark-colored conversion van. The last three numbers of the license plate are four-one-two."

Odell made a face and shook his head. "I've done a lot of work...on a lot of vans."

"Ever put horns and a pitchfork on one of those vans...like a red devil?"

The man hesitated for a split-second. "Don't think so."

Jacob noticed the 'tell,' the flash of recognition in the man's hesitation.

"Need help in here, boss?"

Jacob and Stockwell pivoted their upper bodies toward the doorway, toward the source of the new voice. Two men in coveralls, the two men who were bent over the sedan, stood shoulder-to-shoulder in the hallway.

One was Jacob's height, Latino with dark hair; the other, wiping his hands on a rag, was two inches shorter than Stockwell, Caucasian and sporting a plastered mop of greasy hair.

Odell glimpsed the tall Latino. "No Feliz. These *cops* were just leaving."

Puffing out their chests, the new arrivals stood taller. Greasy entered the office, while Feliz filled the entryway.

Seeing his partner square her hips with the henchmen, Jacob faced Odell. "That's not how this works. *We decide* when we leave. Not you."

Odell tipped his head backward and stared down his nose at Jacob.

Jacob noted the signs; change in posture, nostrils flaring, pupils dilating. The last one was usually difficult to spot, but not at bad breath distances.

"Jake?"

He heard his partner's deeper-than-normal voice, for a woman, drop another octave; a sign her body was prepping. He imagined the men behind him were mirroring Odell's body language. *Are these guys really that dumb to assault FBI agents?* He paused. *Okay one, real FBI agent and one retired.* "Dee."

Hearing his tone, Stockwell knew they were seeing the same thing. Her fingers curled toward her palm. *Why do I have two and he only has one to deal with?* Envisioning Odell's six-six frame, she inwardly huffed. *Albeit one big one though.*

Odell flicked his eyes toward his posse.

Greasy and Feliz glimpsed their boss.

Jacob spotted Odell's chest and stomach muscles contract, as the shop owner slid one foot backward, blading his body. *So this is happening.* He had already sized up his opponent and found a weak spot; the man was top heavy. His legs were too small for his massive upper body. With Stockwell outnumbered, Jacob decided to even the odds.

Jacob put his boot to the side of Odell's forward knee.

The man buckled.

Jacob clamped a hand around his adversary's Adam's apple and shoved.

Odell did a backward somersault, over the desk, crashed into a swivel chair and landed on his back. The chair rolled away.

Pivoting right, Jacob thrust out a foot. The heel of his six-inch 5.11 Tactical boot hit Greasy in the kneecap.

Greasy bent over forward.

Jacob grabbed the man by the shoulders, drove his right knee into the side of Greasy's face, took a step backward and threw him into the rotating office chair behind the desk. He whirled around and spotted the taller man, Feliz, charging his teammate.

...

In one fluid motion, taking a fraction of a second, Stockwell brought her left knee to her chest, jumped into the air and kicked out her right leg; the sole of her chunky high heel connected with Feliz's face, flattening the man's nose.

His head jerking backward, his torso following, the big man dropped to his knees.

Stockwell delivered a right and left cross.

His head whipped one way and then the other.

...

Jacob saw everything. *Dang. She doesn't need my help at all.* He grabbed the chair, pumped his legs and drove the sedentary Greasy into Odell, sending the standing man backpedaling into a wall.

Regaining his senses, the seated man clutched Jacob's leather jacket.

Jacob smacked the man's ears at the same time.

Greasy grabbed his head and hollered.

Seeing Odell's arm coming forward, Jacob lifted Greasy; the man absorbed two blows to the head before Jacob dropped the unconscious employee into the chair.

...

On his knees, Feliz redirected Stockwell's third blow and sunk a fist into her gut.

Embracing her belly, she stumbled backward and collided with a metal file cabinet; a square drawer handle dug into her back. Her inner voice let loose with a few unladylike words.

Rubbing his jaw, Feliz scrambled to his feet.

Holding her lower back, Stockwell rose to her full height.

Feliz wrapped two hands around her neck and squeezed.

She gasped for air.

He lifted her higher.

Rising to the balls of her feet, she yanked on his forearms.

He flexed biceps.

She went to tiptoes.

Feliz pressed harder on her throat.

Stockwell slapped at his arms.

His thumbs pushed her chin up, and backward.

Digging nails into Feliz's skin, she shifted her eyes toward Jacob, who was in a battle of his own. *Jake.* She tried to swallow. *I need you.*

...

Odell swung his fists, over the top of his employee's head.

After one punch grazed his scalp, Jacob blocked another with a forearm before following up with a quick one-two punch. Retreating, he flapped his hand. *Is his head made of stone or what?*

Jacob spotted Stockwell, prying and tugging on the arms that held her in midair, her feet stretching to find solid purchase. He zeroed in on bulging eyes and read her thoughts: *Help.* In his peripheral vision, an incoming fist broke his concentration.

Odell sent out a roundhouse right.

Jacob pitched away, his face scarcely making it out of the arc of the punch. Spying the desk, he picked up a stapler and threw it at Odell, hitting him in the chest. He chucked a container of pens and pencils.

Odell swatted away the writing instruments.

After tossing a few more of the heavier items, Jacob spotted a small clock, set into the face of a softball-sized rock. He grabbed the decorative timepiece and swung his arm, connecting with the side of his opponent's head.

Odell wobbled.

Jacob let go of the granite ornament and barrel-rolled to his left, over the desk. He landed on his feet, kicked the back of Feliz's right knee and grabbed the man's hair with his left hand, right shoulder with the other.

Her feet coming back to the floor, Stockwell broke the chokehold and eyed her partner.

Glimpsing her, Jacob wrenched the man's head back. "Duck."

She listed to one side.

He rammed Feliz's face into the edge of the cabinet. Pulling back for another face plant, focusing on the red smear that had appeared on the beige metal, he noticed his partner.

Stockwell reared up, her left arm cocked.

Jacob cranked his head out of the line of fire.

She delivered a vicious left cross that caught the right corner of Feliz's chin. A sickening crack filled the small office. The man's head whipped counter clockwise, a red string shooting out of his mouth and splattering a nearby window.

Realizing he was supporting all of Feliz's bodyweight, Jacob opened his hands and watched the man crumple to the floor. He came back to her. "Nice." His gaze shot to the right. "Look out!"

Half staggering, bringing his right arm back, Odell advanced toward the agents.

Jacob stepped forward.

Stockwell spun around.

He threw a left.

She threw a right.

Both blows hit Odell in the face, halting his progress. His shoulders sagged.

Getting two handfuls of the heavyweight's shirt, Jacob swiveled right and heaved Odell across the desk.

After clearing the remaining office items from the surface, Odell lay motionless; on his stomach, arms spread wide, limp wrists dangling over the desk's edges, his head hanging over the furniture's far end.

Bending over, Stockwell put one hand on her knee and massaged her throat with the other.

Breathing heavily, Jacob touched her back. "How are you doing?"

"I'll," she coughed, "be," more hacking, "okay." She put a fist to her mouth and coughed several times before clearing her throat. "Thanks Jake. I thought he had me there," she swallowed, "for a second."

After patting her back, Jacob ambled around the desk. He squatted and sat on his haunches in front of Odell.

His eyelids half closed, Odell groaned.

"Now where were we?" Jacob glanced at the floor before lifting his eyes toward the shop owner. "Oh that's right. You were about to tell me the name of the owner of the van with the red devil rims."

Odell met his adversary's penetrating gaze.

Jacob aimed a finger at the man's nose. "Before you even *think* about lying to me...I saw the look on your face. You know who I'm talking about." A beat. "And if," he gave the office an exaggerated look, "our little exercise hasn't convinced you yet," he clamped onto Odell's jaw, pushing the man's cheeks inward, "*I can,* and *I will,* end you...if you feed me a line."

The defeated man gasped and called out a name, a line of spittle coming out as he did so.

Jacob let go of his chin, "Say that again," and wiped the red dots from his hand.

"Vinny," Odell shut his eyes, "Cole."

"Where do I find him?" Jacob slanted sideways and slapped Odell's cheek a couple times. "Hey. Where do I..." he stood and stared at the unconscious man. *Crap.*

"What was that last name?"

He rotated his head toward Stockwell. "Cole."

Hunched over an open file drawer, she thumbed through a few manila folders before pulling out one and reading the label. "Calvin Cole."

Jacob approached her. "Vinny is short for Calvin."

She opened the front flap and perused the file. "It's him...black van with red devil rims."

"Is there an address in there?"

She shuffled papers. "Yup."

"Let's go." Heading for the office door, he stopped and eyed a wall-mounted monitor, which was divided into four separate video feeds. He lifted a hand and waved. A man in the lower left corner mimicked him.

"What's the hold up?"

"There must be a camera in here."

She saw her image on the small LED screen.

"I don't see any wires..." his index finger cut a 'Z' into the air in front of a security system, "or a hard drive. So it must be uploaded to the cloud." He left the office, Stockwell on his heels.

COMING TO THE MAIN area of the garage, Jacob and Stockwell heard the sprayer hissing and saw the same two men working on the same rim. They slipped out of the body shop and climbed into the F-150, slamming doors as their butts hit the seats.

Jacob produced his phone from a jacket pocket, tapped Higs' name on the screen, touched 'speakerphone' and placed the device on the center console.

"Mr. St. Christopher."

"Higs, you're on speaker. Stockwell's with me. I need a cleanup on aisle nine." He leaned forward and ducked to see around his passenger. "Odell's Custom Body Shop...Upper Manhattan...no physical hard drive. We just left there, so scrub all footage from the last hour."

"I'll commence the process straightaway."

"Have you found anything out of place...relating to your friend, Paul Gentry?"

"Not as of yet; however, algorithms have only just begun to scour the Internet."

Jacob eyed his partner, who was rifling through the contents of the file folder, snapping pictures of documents with her mobile. "We have a lead, a name from the owner of the body shop...Calvin 'Vinny' Cole. We're going to pay him a visit."

"And was this body shop owner cooperative in

providing you with the name of this Mr. Calvin Cole?"

Stockwell stopped taking pictures to glance at Jacob. Grinning at her, Jacob hesitated. "*Very* cooperative."

She shook her head and went back to her work.

"I see."

Jacob attached his seatbelt. "For expediency's sake, however, you should probably just delete the security footage." Out of the corner of his eye, he saw Stockwell crack a smile. "No sense wasting your time reviewing it." He started the truck's engine. "Stockwell will be sending you information on Cole. If you come up with anything interesting, let us know."

"Very good, Mr. St. Christopher."

Jacob scooped his phone off the console.

"By the way, Ms. Stockwell?"

"Yeah Higs?"

"How are you feeling? Specifically...your *throat*, I mean."

Holding her cell above the folder, her index finger hovering over the digital shutter button, she frowned at the phone in the driver's hand.

Jacob cocked his head. "So you've already seen the video?"

"Indeed."

She chuckled. "I'm fine, Higs. No need to worry."

"I'm glad to hear it." A moment passed. "And for what it's worth, that left cross was exquisite."

She smiled. "Thank you."

"I'll be in contact the second I have new information to pass along."

"Thanks Higs." Jacob disconnected the call, ran the gearshift to 'D' and peeled away from the curb. Minutes later, he navigated the Ford onto Interstate 95, heading north.

Stockwell closed the file and sent the pictures to Higs.

One hand on the steering wheel, the other scratching his chin, Jacob peeked at her. "So that jump kick...where'd you learn to do something like that?"

She tipped her head back and massaged her neck muscles. "When I was a kid, I—" rubbing a tender spot, she winced, "I wanted to be a gymnast." She looked out her window. "Turns out, I was too tall. Shorter people tend to have a better power-to-weight ratio." She shrugged. "So I pivoted. I decided I wanted to become a dancer instead."

"Really?"

"I took lessons for three years. Got pretty good at it too. Then, I had another growth spurt. My arms and legs developed minds of their own. I stumbled, fumbled and tripped through dance moves I had done hundreds of times before."

A half-mile of Jacob stealing glimpses of her went by. "So what happened?"

She studied her fingernails for a few thoughtful moments. "I," her voice was a whisper, "eventually had to give up my dream."

More miles passed. Jacob watched her fiddle with her nails. "You really wanted to be a dancer, didn't you?"

For several seconds, she stared at her fingers. Her shoulders rising and falling one time, she let out a quick sigh. "That's life. Anyway," she tipped her head backward, toward the scene of the fight, "I guess I still remember a few of those moves."

Jacob nodded. "And that left cross back there...you knocked that guy out cold. Did they teach you that in dance school?"

"No," Stockwell smiled, "that came after another *pivot point* in my life. I took up boxing."

His eyes popping, "What?" the driver pivoted his head a couple times, his attention going back and forth from his female companion to the traffic ahead. "You can box too?"

"Undefeated in ten bouts."

"Okay Stockwell," Jacob squared his shoulders with her as much as he could, while keeping his eyes on the road, "this is the kind of stuff you *need* to be telling me."

She faced him. "I only boxed for a few years."

"I don't care. This is cool." He rolled a hand. "Tell me more."

"Cool? Tell that to the boys at my high school. None of them wanted anything to do with a girl who was tougher than they were. My prom date always ended up being a shorter, squirrely kid. Every slow dance, his nose was sandwiched between my boobs."

Jacob looked away, suppressing laughter.

"When the song was over, his glasses were all fogged up."

Jacob smiled. "Just goes to show you...there are advantages to everything."

"Funny. Anyway...back to boxing...there wasn't much of a demand for girl fighters. There were only a handful of us. In fact, we ended up fighting each other a couple times over."

"Still," he shot out a puff of air, "*undefeated...that's awesome.*" He slowly shook his head. "Wow."

"Yeah, when I hit my late teens, I finally grew into this," she ran a hand over the length of her body, "*beautiful specimen* you see before you."

Jacob chuckled.

"I learned being tall was an advantage for a boxer. My coach taught me how to generate power from my legs. And my long arms kept the other fighters at bay." She raised her balled hands and extended her right fist a few times. "I would bop them on the nose over and over and over again."

Jacob smiled.

"Then, after I wore them down," her left fist shot outward, "I started landing the left crosses."

"Any knockouts?"

"Only technicals." She laughed quietly. "I don't think people really wanted to see a girl get knocked unconscious...and fall to the mat like a tree in the forest. The referees were quick to call the matches."

"Well," Jacob bobbed his head backward, "I'll bet that guy back there would've welcomed a referee."

She sniggered.

Jacob passed a car and navigated into the right lane. "So I have to know." He gave her a quick look and curled up a corner of his mouth.

Hearing his tone and seeing the smirk, she turned her upper body toward him and crossed arms over her chest, expecting a playful, off-color remark.

"Circling back to dancing," he hesitated, "are you telling me you can do one of those sexy leg kicks they do on those dance shows?"

Stockwell lifted an eyebrow at her man.

"You know where—"

"You mean," she half grinned, "circling back to *sex*."

He let out a short snicker, "You know where the woman puts the back of her ankle on the man's shoulder," he gestured, "almost like a...a," he peered at her legs, "standing leg split?"

Smiling, she barely shook her head at him. "Does everything always come back to sex with you?"

He lifted his shoulder. "I do try to be consistent."

She laughed and faced forward. "Well I guess you'll just have to take me dancing to find out."

His eyes going down and up her figure, Jacob envisioned his woman in a slinky dress and high heels. He leveled a finger at her. "You're on, Stockwell."

4:51 P.M.

Zoe wrapped her shirt around the high heel shoe several times. She was careful not to cushion the spike too much. Aiming for the pane's center, she brought back the footwear and shot a downward glance over her shoulder. "Watch yourself, Ay."

On all fours, Zoe's feet pressing on her back, the older sibling closed her eyes and hung her head. "Okay. Do it."

Zoe swung the heel; the tip of the spike hit the window. She delivered two more blows, each one progressively harder, louder. Her heart beating faster, she whipped her head around and spied the door to their prison cell.

"What's going on up there?"

"It won't break."

"Are you using the spike part?"

"*Of course I'm—*" Zoe shot back before taking a quick breath and blowing out the air through pursed lips. "Okay, I just have to nail it. Watch yourself." She reared back and threw forward her arm; the high heel connected with the window.

The sound of breaking glass filled the room's interior.

Freezing in place, holding her shoe—which was half inside and half outside the basement—Zoe brought her shoulders up to her neck and winced.

Ayda's body tensed.

For several long seconds, neither woman moved a muscle. The door remained closed. No footsteps came from the other side.

Ayda lifted her head and spied the stronger beam of light, penetrating the dark cellar. "Do you think they heard that?"

Zoe's shoulders fell. "I think we're good." She knocked out the rest of the glass and ran her shoe around the sill, clearing away sharp edges before stepping off her human platform.

Ayda stood and arched her back. "Okay, make me a foothold."

Bent over, ankle on knee, wiggling her shoe back onto her foot, Zoe looked up and shook her head. "We've been over this. I'm the one going."

"You've done enough already. I should be the one to go for help."

Zoe stood erect and hiked her skirt's hem above her waist to protect her torso from glass shards. "And what if you have another attack?"

"I have the inhaler."

Zoe dropped a hand onto her big sister's shoulder. "I got this, Ay. Don't worry. I'll find help and be back as soon as I can." She jabbed a finger at Ayda. "Just take it easy and try to stay calm. You hear me?"

Ayda flashed a fading smile, glanced at the floor and regarded Zoe. "*I'm supposed to be the one taking care of you, remember?*"

"Let me carry the ball for a while." She tossed her shirt over the lower part of the windowsill and stared at the garment. "That should protect me..." her eyebrows bobbed once, "somewhat...hopefully."

"Be careful, Zo Zo."

Zoe grinned. "I always am."

Rolling her eyes, "Yeah right," Ayda squatted and interlaced her fingers, making a foothold.

Zoe put the sole of her shoe on the makeshift step. Grabbing the sill and pulling, while thrusting out her right leg, she launched her body up and through the short, wide opening.

Holding her sister's feet, Ayda struggled to provide the opposite force to Zoe's kicks.

On her belly, her head and shoulders out of the window, wrists crossed in front of her, Zoe gingerly placed elbows on the hardpan earth. "Ouch." She lifted her right arm and pulled out the one-inch jagged piece of glass from her forearm; blood trickled down her arm.

Ayda pushed.

Zoe slithered over the sill, feeling the unprotected skin between her front bra strap and her skirt scraping across bits of glass. Cringing, she planted elbows on the ground, hoisted her torso and wriggled her shoulders back and forth. More cuts developed on her arms.

Ayda pushed.

Zoe squirmed forward, the back of her bra strap pulling away from her body.

Ayda shoved.

Zoe inched her way outside, the strain around her midsection growing. Staring at the dirt, her face twisted, her body tensing, she wriggled along on her elbows, waiting for the elastic band to smack her between the shoulder blades.

A muffled scream came from inside.

Zoe lifted her head. "Ayda?" Her sister's slender fingers were replaced by two sets of rough, calloused hands, each pair closing around an ankle. "Ayd—"

Zoe's feet hit the hard surface first before she landed on her butt and elbow. An instant tingling, burning sensation flooded the joint. Screwing up her face, cradling the injured elbow, she rolled onto her back and cried out in pain.

"Zoe!" Ayda darted toward her sister.

Clown 1 clutched her by the throat and threw her into the corner near the window. Her right shoulder and right temple hit the cinder blocks.

Zoe lifted her head and spotted her sister's crumpled and still form. "Ayd—" more pain sent her head back to the concrete. Her feet on the floor, her legs forming two, upside down V's, she rolled back and forth onto each hip, throwing out her knees in unison, while sobbing, nursing the bad arm. Above her, two clown-faced men came into view.

Clown 2 and Clown 3 turned her onto her stomach and yanked both arms behind her back.

Zoe lifted her head and yelled.

Clown 2 bound her wrists.

Clown 3 crossed her ankles before binding them.

Still bellowing, her chest heaving, she touched her cheek to the dirty floor.

The men secured her wrists and ankles together, lifted her, and carried her toward the doorway.

Her head hanging down, Zoe looked right; Ayda was bound in the same way, a black hood over her head. The pain in Zoe's arm grew in intensity with each up and down movement, each bounce. The gray floor zipped by, inches from her nose. She shut her eyes. A few moments later, she blacked out.

5:43 P.M.
QUEENS, NEW YORK

Jacob steered the F-150 toward the curb, parking the Ford several houses down from the target house, Cole's house. The driver killed the engine and looked out his window.

With no yard whatsoever in this overcrowded neighborhood, the single-story home was in decent condition. To the dwelling's right, to the east, further down the street, was an abandoned convenience store. A chain-link fence—tall grass growing beside, and within, the barrier—separated the properties. A similarly modest residence sat west of Cole's house, a one-car driveway between the two structures.

Stockwell pivoted in her seat, spying the foot traffic, before facing forward. "People are coming home. They're starting to gather on the porches."

In the side mirror, Jacob viewed the scene behind him. "Hopefully," he gazed straight ahead, "this won't come to guns."

"If they have Ayda and Zoe in there...it'll come to guns."

"I said *hopefully.*"

"So," the word was a complete sentence. "Our usual entry?"

Squinting at the darkened windows of Cole's place, he knew what she meant. After gaining entry, she would cover left and low; he would take high and right. It was their thing, originating from their first raid together when they were searching for Jacob's soon-to-be—in every practical sense—adopted daughter, Amanda. "As much as I hate to be away from you, Stockwell, we need to breach quickly and find the girls." He removed two communication earpieces from the center console and gave one to her. "I think we should split up."

"I see." She inserted the bud into her ear. "The story of my life. Men just can't handle me, so they end the relationship."

Facing her, while inserting his comm, he showed a half grin. "You haven't given me the chance yet. Maybe *you* won't be able to handle," he hesitated, "what *I* have to offer."

Shouldering open her door, she matched his expression and added a raised eyebrow. "I can only hope that's true."

Chuckling to himself, Jacob exited the truck, grabbed his soft armor vest from the metal box in the backseat and met her at the passenger side. He took off his jacket, and donned and secured the vest, "Okay," before rolling his shoulders, "that verbal foreplay got the blood pumping."

Chortling to herself, Stockwell swung open the rear door.

He retrieved a similar vest from her side of the box. "I had these specially made for us. Mine accommodates my shoulder holster, while yours..."

She slipped off her three-quarter-sleeve suit coat.

"...accommodates your," he pumped cupped hands in front of his pectoral muscles, "*unique assets.*"

She took the protective clothing from him. "Is that what we're calling them these days?"

"It should be more comfortable than what you're used to wearing."

"I'm curious. You lifted my fingerprints from drinking glasses...for this secret stash of weapons and gear. What did you use for my chest measurements?"

"My imagination."

She stuck one hand through an armhole, stopped and arched an eyebrow at him. "Is that so? And I thought you were going to say you rifled through my underwear drawer and peeked at one of my bras."

"I suppose that," he put on his jacket, while staring beyond her shoulder, "would've been simpler." A twinkle materialized in his eye. "But my method was more fun."

Sniggering, "Well," she shrugged into the vest and attached the side straps, "I'm sure my...*unique assets* will thank you for the comfort."

Jacob flashed a smile before jutting out his chin at the garment. "That's made from a new, high-end ballistic material. It has level three-A protection, but thirty percent less bulk and weight." He plucked her coat from the front seat. "Turn around."

Stockwell pivoted and lifted her straight arms a short ways behind her back.

"It'll..." he married the jacket's inside sleeve openings with her hands and slid the garment over her shoulders, "stop all common pistol calibers."

She flattened the collar. "Thanks."

He slammed both doors, and they walked to the truck's front bumper. "Let's do this." He faced her. "Ladies' choice...do you prefer the front door or the back door?"

A mischievous smile formed on her face.

The expression reminded him of their earlier, double entendre conversation. Crossing the street, shaking his head, "I'm sensing," he poked a finger at her, "a naughty side to your personality, Stockwell."

"I call it *playful*." Shoulder-to-shoulder, they strode down the sidewalk. "At the risk of miscommunication," she paused, "later on in this relationship that is...I prefer the back door."

Jacob tapped his temple with the side of an index finger. "I'll file that away for future reference."

She snickered, veered left and walked up the driveway to the left of Cole's house.

"Hey."

She turned toward him.

"Let me know when you've gained entry."

"I will."

"But don't go in."

She nodded.

Ascending the porch steps, Jacob stole glances up and down the street; kids were filling the sidewalks—carrying toys, walking bikes. Grownups were exiting cars—holding briefcases, clutching purses. *Sure don't...* he approached the front door, *want this...* and peeked through the window on the right, *to come to guns.*

Grabbing the butt of his Coonan 357, he eased the screen door open and tried the doorknob; it rotated. He pushed the door inward a hair and waited.

. . .

Peeling back the right lapel of her suit coat, Stockwell clamped down on the Glock on her waistband. She lifted a gate's latch, slipped through the opening and fast walked to the back door. Scanning the remote area surrounding the back of the house, she saw no one.

Reaching behind her, she discovered the door was locked. She pivoted, eyed the barrier and tapped her earpiece. "Jake," her voice was low, "I'm in position. Door's locked." She spied the glass above the round handle. "I can break a window and have it open in no time."

"Copy that. We go on your order. Break it, get in and find the girls."

Stockwell drew her weapon and put the butt to the

lower left corner of the pane. "Get ready." She smashed the glass, made an opening big enough for her hand and unlocked the door. "I'm in. Go, go, go."

. . .

Gun up, Jacob rushed into the house, glanced right, sidestepped in the same direction and swung his 1911 to the left. He spotted Stockwell at the other end of the living room.

Stockwell spied her partner.

He sliced the air to his left.

Glimpsing a closed door to her right, she nodded.

Jacob snaked around furniture, pivoted right and crept down a hallway. He cleared a bathroom and two bedrooms before meeting his teammate between the living room and the dining area.

She bobbed her head backward. "Room's clear."

"I saw a window at ground level. You see any doors leading to a basement?"

She jerked her head toward the back of the house. "Kitchen."

He dashed forward, Stockwell right behind him. Aiming his firearm at the interior door, he caught her attention and dipped his forehead toward the handle.

She rushed ahead.

He lowered the Coonan's muzzle, as she crossed in front of him.

Stockwell grabbed the doorknob and looked back.

Having retrieved a Pelican 1920B flashlight from a

pocket, he nodded.

She stepped backward and pulled open the door.

Lifting the 357 Magnum ninety degrees, Jacob leaned left, lit up the basement stairs and the immediate area below. "Clear." He moved forward. "Stay on my six."

"Copy."

He descended the staircase, stopping every third plank to thumb the flashlight's rubber boot and illuminate the darkness. He scanned the cellar as it came into view with each downward step.

Coming to the concrete floor, Jacob pivoted left and viewed a short, empty hallway with an open door on the right. He crept forward and looked over his shoulder, at his teammate.

Stockwell made eye contact.

With his left hand, he chopped the nine o'clock air before making a sweeping motion, down and outward.

Her mind interpreting the signals, she nodded. *And you'll cover high and right.*

Jacob took sideways baby steps. Exposing little of himself to potential incoming fire, he 'sliced the pie' and cleared most of the dimly lit space.

Standing on opposite sides of the doorway, the aim of their pistols crisscrossing, the duo acknowledged each other.

"Go!" Jacob curled around the jamb and darted right.

She entered the area and swung her Glock left. "Clear."

"Clear." Jacob holstered the 357 and shone his light in all directions before making a beeline for a window. After glancing down, he pointed at the rectangular opening above. "It was broken from the inside." He plucked a woman's blouse from the sill, and unhooked a black bra, caught on a metal latch.

"I got blood over here."

Examining the garments, he spun toward her.

Down on her haunches, she shined her flashlight on the floor in front of her. "A few droplets, but most of it's been smeared...as if...someone was dragged a few inches."

Jacob held up the shirt. "What color were the blouses Mrs. Gentry said her daughters were wearing?"

Stockwell stood and continued eyeing the floor. "Police reports said she wasn't certain, but," Jacob's partner faced him, "she was pretty sure Zoe's was light in color...white, maybe cream."

Jacob lifted the smooth material a little higher. "I'd say this falls into that color palette."

She observed the window beyond his shoulder. "Do you think the women were here?"

"I'm not sure, but," he gestured at the evidence, in succession, "women's clothing, broken glass, blood on the floor...*something* happened here." He forfeited the attire and shined the Pelican at the far corners of the basement, stopping when the beam hit the corner left of the window. Tipping his head to one side, and squinting, Jacob marched to the corner, stooped and picked up a white object. He frowned at the L-shaped plastic item for several seconds. "Hey Stockwell..."

She looked his way.

Turning toward her, he brought the item to eye level. "Didn't the police report say that Ayda's inhaler was found where the women were taken?"

Stockwell approached and took the inhaler from him. "Yes, it did." She examined the device.

"So," Jacob pointed, "how did *that* get here?"

"The homeowner has asthma too?"

"Maybe." He folded his arms across his chest and rubbed his temples with a thumb and middle finger.

"We really have no idea what went on here, Jake." She motioned. "This is all circumstantial evidence. For all we know, the asthmatic homeowner—*Cole*—broke a window and cut himself in the process of cleaning up the mess."

Washing a hand down his face, Jacob stopped, cupped his chin and regarded her. "While wearing a bra and a slinky blouse?"

"Maybe a woman lives here with him."

Jacob lowered hands to his hips. "We have an eye witness that saw a dark van with red devil rims. We've all but confirmed the owner of that van—Calvin Cole—lives here...*where* we find evidence of possible foul play. Add an asthma inhaler and that circumstantial evidence becomes more damning."

"Okay," Stockwell pumped a hand toward him, "let's go with that for a moment...that the kidnappers brought the women here." She paused. "How did they know they would need an inhaler when they abducted Ayda and Zoe?"

Jacob narrowed his eyes at her. "We're back to my theory again."

After a moment of reflection, Stockwell slowly shook her head. "That's a pretty big leap. We're going to need solid proof to make an accusation like that."

He pointed his forehead at the things she held. "We just might have a way to get that proof." Crossing in front of her, he gently squeezed her upper arm, "Let's go," before heading for the doorway. "We have a party to crash."

7:07 P.M.
MIDTOWN MANHATTAN

Jacob thrust out his Homeland Security credentials. "*Here's* my invitation. Now kindly point us toward the dinner party..." he spied the slim name placard on the woman's white dress shirt, "Ms. Stephenson."

The twenty-something's eyes grew bigger when she saw the badge. "It's...it's," she extended her left arm and pivoted her head in the same direction, "right down the main hall, through the double doors."

"Thank you." Jacob strode away from the reception desk.

Stockwell caught up to him. "It might be best if you didn't come in hot, Jake. You can always get mad later, but it's hard to back down from that starting point."

He whipped out his hands, palms up. "Who's mad? I'm not mad. I'm," he hesitated, "determined...to find Ayda and Zoe."

"So am I, but we need to go about this wisely."

"I know exactly what I'm doing, Stockwell."

She shot him a sideways glance. "I know you do. That's what has me worried."

Jacob threw open both doors and marched forward.

The opulent dining area had tall plants in every corner and chandeliers hanging from the ceiling. At the far end, a man stopped speaking in mid-sentence.

Stockwell peered at the partygoers. Men in black suits, women in evening gowns, sat at round tables, which were finely decorated with fancy crystal dinnerware and white linens that almost touched the burgundy carpet. Counting six tables on both sides of a main walkway, eight people at each dining station, she did the math. She and Jacob had the attention of close to a hundred sets of eyes.

Jacob never lost a step.

Even with her long legs, Stockwell found herself half skipping every third or fourth step to keep pace with him. Noticing women lean closer to their male companions, while covering their mouths with a hand, she imagined the questions: *What's going on, Herbert? Who are they? What are they doing here?* Her skin tingling, her stomach muscles tightening, Stockwell answered. *Hopefully, not making a bad career move.*

Jacob halted at the head table, situated perpendicular to the round ones he had passed. Standing directly in front of a seated Paul Gentry, he acknowledged the man's wife. "Mrs. Gentry, I apologize for the intrusion, but," he turned back to Gentry, "I need to have a word with your husband...in private."

Gentry glimpsed his investors, "What's this..." before facing Jacob, "all about? Have you found something?"

"You could say that." Jacob removed his hand from his leather jacket.

Gentry scowled at the inhaler Jacob held. "I'm not following."

Jacob studied the man, but his opponent showed no telltale signs of lying. "How about we continue this elsewhere?"

Gentry sighed and stood. "I'll be right back, dear."

Lisa Gentry scooted her chair backward.

"Ma'am," Jacob lifted a hand toward her, "it might be better if you stayed here."

"If this has something to do with my daughters, I want to hear it." She rose from her chair and tossed a cloth napkin onto her plate. "I never wanted to come to this thing anyway."

"Honey...please."

"Paul," she held a finger in the air between her and her husband, "you know I hate it when you take that tone with me."

"All right," he hugged her shoulders, "all right," and pivoted her away from the table, while eyeing his guests. "Let's talk about this in private." He escorted his wife into a small room—dark-colored paneling, red carpet, one couch and sparse decorations—off the main banquet area. Gentry closed the door after Jacob and Stockwell entered. "Now what's this all about?"

Squaring off with Ayda and Zoe's father, Stockwell on his four o'clock, Jacob raised the asthma medication again. "So this doesn't look familiar to you?"

"It's an inhaler." Gentry shrugged. "What do you want me to say? They're everywhere. Lots of people use them."

"This was found at a home in Queens..." Jacob paused, thinking he had seen the man twitch, "along with a bra and a woman's shirt. We think your daughters were held captive at the house."

Standing a few feet to her husband's left, wearing high heels, a navy blue dress, and a white shawl draped around her shoulders, Lisa drew closer to the men. "Have you found them? Have you found my children?"

Jacob faced her. "No, ma'am, but I'm hoping Mr. Gentry can help with that."

"Paul?" She glimpsed her husband and came back to the male agent. "How?"

"Yes," Gentry crossed his arms over his chest and stood taller, "just how do you think I can help? I've already told the police, the FBI," he stuck out his chin, "*you...everything I know.*"

Jacob gritted his teeth and narrowed his eyes at the man.

Feeling, more than seeing, his expression, Stockwell took a half step toward her partner.

"So I'm curious," Gentry rocked backward, onto his heels, and studied the floor before eyeing the taller man, "what further information could I possibly have that could help you find my daughters?"

Jacob gripped the inhaler tighter. "I'm done playing games with you."

Stockwell slipped her fingers around her man's elbow. "Jake."

He wagged the medical device at Gentry. "Did you buy this?" His voice was gruff, louder. "Did you give this to the kidnappers before they took Ayda and Zoe?"

Her fingertips going to her chest, Lisa gasped.

His upper body becoming rigid, Gentry separated his intertwined forearms a few inches. "Excuse me?"

"Mr. St. Christopher," Lisa stepped between him and her spouse, "you better have a damn good reason for suggesting my husband had anything to do with this."

Jacob hauled out the black bra and light-colored shirt. "Do these look familiar?"

The Gentry's examined the clothing. "No," he said.

"Should we?" she said. "Are these the things you said you found at the home...in Queens?" She took the lingerie and blouse.

"I've had enough of this." Gentry produced his phone. "I'm calling the FBI." He leveled a finger at the agents. "I'm having you removed from this case. In fact, I'm pressing charges against both of you."

"So," Jacob's gaze penetrated to the back of Gentry's head, "if we were to contact the pharmacies in New York, none of them would have a record of you filling a prescription for an asthma inhaler? And before you answer, know this...we can—"

"Paul," Lisa gaped at the blouse, "this is Zoe's."

Jacob and Stockwell faced the woman. "How do you know that?" he said.

"They're identical twins. They usually end up liking the same stuff. Ever since they were kids—old enough to write their names—they've always written on the tags of their clothing." Her hands trembling, she lifted the garment higher and peered at her husband. "It has Zo Zo's 'Z' on the tag." The mother's lower lip quivered. "And it has," her voice cracked, "blood on it."

Staring at the shirt's red stains, Gentry disconnected the call.

"Maybe now you can explain to me, Mr. Gentry," Jacob motioned toward the inhaler, "how the medicine your daughter needs to live," he paused, "just so happens to be with her...*when we know...Ayda's inhaler* was found at the scene of the abduction."

Curling a finger inside his collar and twisting his head from side to side, Gentry tugged on the tie knot.

Noting her man's wrinkled upper lip and twitching cheek muscles, Lisa spoke in between whimpers. "Paul...what's...going on?"

Stowing his mobile, he shifted his gaze toward her.

She wiped her eyes. "I," she sniffed, "I know that look."

Running thumbs back and forth inside the waistband of his trousers, he hiked his pants.

She squared her shoulders with him and slowly shook

her head. "What have you done?"

Gentry put one hand on his hip, turned around and rubbed the back of his neck.

"Look at me, Paul." Lisa's voice had returned; it was deeper. "What did you do?"

Hanging his head, he shut his eyes and pinched the bridge of his nose. "It wasn't supposed to happen this way?"

"Oh my—" the clothing falling from her hands, Lisa covered her mouth, stretched out an arm and teetered away from the others.

Jacob darted between Stockwell and Gentry and caught the falling woman.

Gentry leaped forward. "That's my wife. Don't you touch her."

One arm around her shoulders, the other holding her hand, Jacob whipped his head toward the man. "Are you really going to play that card right now?"

Noticing the fire in Jacob's eyes, Gentry froze in place before backtracking.

"Give me a hand, Stockwell."

Stockwell took Lisa's other arm, and the agents helped her to the couch.

"Stay with her." He bolted toward Gentry.

Gentry backpedaled, until he collided with a wall.

Stockwell curled an arm around the crying, grieving woman and patted her forearm. "Try to stay calm, Mrs. Gentry. Jake and I will find Ayda and Zoe. You have to believe that. You have to believe that your kids are still okay."

Jacob stopped a few inches from the sweating man. If he leaned forward, the two could have kissed. "Where are the girls?"

"I don't know."

"What do you mean you don't know? You set this whole thing up."

"That was before."

"Before what?"

"They called me—the kidnappers—demanding more money; a half a million. They were supposed to care for my daughters. The plan was for me to pay the original ransom, and a couple days after this dinner party, they were to release them...unharmed." Gentry wiped his brow. "They would wear masks and never speak, so Ayda and Zoe would never be able to identify them."

"Why Paul?" Lisa started to stand, but Stockwell stopped her. "Why would you kidnap our girls?"

He leaned right, around Jacob, and beheld his wife. "The year-end financial statements were coming out. The company was set to lose more than five hundred million dollars...due to a glitch in the security software."

"That's what this is about?" screamed Lisa. "*Money?*"

"I knew I could fix it, but I was going to need more time," he paused, "and yes...more money." He glimpsed Jacob, "I thought if I distracted the investors from the financials," before he came back to his wife, "I could get an infusion of capital and save the business. No one could say 'no' to a man, whose kids were taken from him." He shook his head. "But it was never supposed to come to this."

Jacob locked eyes with the man. "That was the call you took...when we were at your house, wasn't it? The kidnappers were squeezing you for more money."

Gentry nodded. "That was the second call. The first one—demanding the new amount—took place a day ago. I don't have that kind of money. I told them 'yes,' but I...I was just hoping," his bottom lip twitched, "*you'd* find them first...and bring my daughters back home."

"So you conned your friend, Higs, into getting involved. You knew he'd send someone to help..." seeing Stockwell in his mind, Jacob bobbed his head backward, "*us.*"

Gentry screwed up his face. Water gathered at the corners of his eyes. "I didn't know what else to do."

Jacob gripped Gentry's jacket lapels and pushed him into the wall. "You don't get to cry." He jammed his finger into the man's chest. "You did this. Suck it up."

Gentry swallowed, sniffed and rubbed his eyes.

"The man you've been in contact with...what's his name?"

"He went by Vinny."

"Calvin 'Vinny' Cole?"

Gentry shook his head. "I don't know his name. I told you. All he ever said was Vinny."

"Where was he supposed to keep the girls?"

"Somewhere in the city...at his house I think."

Jacob's clenched fist, still grasping a lapel, pressed on Gentry's Adam's apple. "How many kidnappers are there?"

"I—" Gentry coughed, "I don't know."

Jacob's balled hand pushed harder. "What number did he call you from?"

Jumping to her feet, "Stay here, Mrs. Gentry," Stockwell hurried toward the men.

Gentry gurgled out his next words. "I...don't...know."

"Jake." Stockwell forced her arms between the grappling men.

Jacob held firm. "Damn it, Gentry..."

"Jake," she wiggled her body forward.

"...give me something I can use."

"Jacob Samuel," barked Stockwell.

He faced her. Moments passed. After another glance at the man, he let go and faced her.

Scowling, she lowered her voice. "That's enough."

Bending over, coughing, Gentry massaged his throat and turned his head from side to side. "It," he coughed, "came up as an unknown number. I tried calling it...several times. It's," he hacked, "no longer in service."

Putting a hand on his hip, Jacob spun around and ran fingers through his hair before wringing the back of his neck. "So your *fake*, theatrical kidnapping has now turned into a *real* one."

Taking his elbow, Stockwell put her left shoulder to his left pectoral muscle and sloped toward him. "Jake," she whispered in his ear. "You need to cool off. This isn't helping find Ayda and Zoe. You need to calm down.

Don't focus on," she stuck out her thumb toward Gentry, "this guy. Focus on the girls, the Innocents."

Jacob stood erect, filled his lungs, and squinted at the ceiling for a few seconds. *She's right.* "You're right. We need to make a move. We need to know where the kidnappers took them." He paused. "We need to find that black van. We find that...and we find the girls." He retrieved his cell phone.

"Who are you calling?"

He put the mobile to his ear. "It's time Higs knows the truth," he glimpsed Gentry, "about his *friend.*"

. . .

7:21 P.M.
STATEN ISLAND, NEW YORK
ST. GEORGE NEIGHBORHOOD
"THE KEEP"

Jacob: "Higs? Higs, you still there?"

In the conference room, slouched in a high-back leather chair, Higs held his forehead, not hearing Jacob's voice anymore. Having heard Paul Gentry, his long-time friend, was responsible for Ayda and Zoe's kidnapping, Higs shut down mentally.

"Talk to me, buddy."

The computer guru slowly ran his hand down his face before picking up his eyeglasses. "I'm here." Sliding the bows over his ears, he slipped on the spectacles. "I'm here, Mr. St. Christopher. I hear you."

"You okay?"

"Yes," Higs faltered, "I will be." He pecked at the

laptop keys. "I'll begin retrieving video feeds from cameras in the area around Mr. Cole's residence. Do you have a possible window of time for me, Mr. St. Christopher?"

"Stockwell said the blood on the floor was almost dry, so if my calculations are correct, we arrived no more than an hour after the kidnappers left."

Higs checked the time on his computer. "I'll add a thirty-minute cushion to the search radius and take into consideration," he typed, "the different speed limits of the major routes leading away from the nucleus," more typing, "and factor in time delays for the influx of five o'clock commuters..."

. . .

MIDTOWN MANHATTAN

Jacob rolled his eyes at Stockwell, as he listened to Higs drone on about algorithms, computations, factoring. "Sounds great, Higs. That's exactly what I would do too. Let us know as soon as you have something concrete."

"You have my word."

"We're ready to move. We just need you to tell us where to go." He paused. In his ear, he heard a keyboard being worked. "The longer this plays out, Higs, the more emboldened the kidnappers will become."

"I know."

"Increasing the ransom demand suggests they're upping the stakes. They're taking more ris—"

          ABOVE & BEYOND

"I'm well aware of the urgency of the matter, Mr. St. Christopher."

Hearing a tone he had never heard from his boss, Jacob backtracked. "Okay…"

"If there's nothing further, I have a lot of work to do."

"…okay, just get back to me when you have something." He started to tap the 'end' icon, but stopped when he noticed Higs had already ended the call.

Stockwell came in close and whispered to her partner. "How's he doing?"

"He's rattled."

She pursed her lips and nodded. "Understandable. He knows the Innocents, *personally*."

Jacob poked his chin at Gentry. "What do we do with him?"

After a quick look at the man-in-question's pale cheeks, sweat-stained shirt and loosened tie, she stretched out a hand. "I'll call the bureau…"

Jacob forfeited his phone.

"…and get a couple agents to escort him back to his house—and watch him—until this is over." Stockwell tapped the screen several times and put the device to her ear. "We may still need him…if the kidnappers make contact again." She turned her back on Jacob. "This is Special Agent Stockwell. I need a two-man detail sent to…"

Jacob flicked his eyes in the other direction, toward Lisa. *She shouldn't be alone right now.* He sat next to the woman. "Mrs. Gentry, is there anyone you'd like us to call...to come get you, to stay with you?"

"No." Her face buried in her palms, elbows on knees, she shook her head. "I'm fine."

"With all due respect, ma'am, you shouldn't be alone at a time like this."

"She won't be alone." Gentry approached from his spot near the wall. "She'll be with *me*."

Lisa jumped up from the couch before Jacob could catch her. She rushed across the room and pounded on her husband's chest. Curse words intermingled with screams and cries.

Stockwell whirled around and grabbed one of Lisa's wrists.

Curling an arm around the elder female's stomach, Jacob drew the mother of two away from Gentry and escorted her back to the couch. "Please ma'am...who would you like me to call for you?"

7:41 P.M.

Ayda tipped the water bottle.

Feeling the cold liquid hit the open wound on her bare back, Zoe twitched, shut her eyes and pounded on the bed frame. "*Damn...*" wincing, she turned her head to the side, "*it.*"

Ayda dabbed the area around the six-inch gash with a dingy, off-white pillowcase. "Sorry, but we need to keep this as clean as possible."

"I know. I know."

"That window," Ayda softly blew on her sister's laceration, "did a number on your back."

Zoe held her arm and rolled her shoulder.

Ayda offered the bottle. "How's your elbow doing?"

"The pain's subsided, but," Zoe took a swig, "my joints are stiff."

Ayda thought of the long drive to this new location, both of them hogtied in the back of a van. "Tell me about it." Sitting on the bed, next to her sister, she rubbed her knees. "My whole body aches."

"Look on the bright side." After finishing off the rest of the water, the younger sibling stood. "At least our accommodations have been upgraded." She dropped the plastic container and wrapped a wool blanket around her naked torso. "We're," she made a face when the coarse fabric scraped across her injury, "no longer in a basement."

The women were in a ten-by-ten room with a twin-sized bed in one corner. Power bars and bottled water were scattered on a small table that sat against a wall, halfway between the bed and a door. One boarded-up window was on the other side of the bed. Tiny cracks between planks let in no light. The rest of the space was barren, except for a table lamp on the floor, in the middle of the room.

"And..." ambling toward the door, careful not to slide her bare feet over the rough, wooden floorboards, Zoe nodded at the lamp, "we now have a heater."

"Where are you going?"

"I have to pee." She banged on the door with a flat hand. "Hey...anybody out there?" After listening to silence for a few seconds, she hit the door again. "Hey, I have to pee. Can someone open the door?" A beat. "Anyone?" More time passed. "Come on. I just—"

A latch turned and the door swung outward. Two men in clown masks stood on the other side.

"Thank you." She took a step.

Clown 1 stopped her with a stiff arm.

Looking through the mask's oblong openings, she peered into the eyes behind.

He dipped his head toward her and motioned with

his hands.

She frowned. "What? What do you want?"

He ripped apart the ends of the blanket.

Wearing only her skirt, Zoe folded arms over her bare breasts. "What the hell?"

He gave her a quick, visible search, let go of the covering and beckoned her with a wave of an arm.

Closing the material around her body again, she followed him.

Clown 2 trudged behind her after locking the door.

Passing through a large room, she gawked out a bay window; the area beyond was dark. Moonlight showed a thick forest of trees.

Clown 2 shoved her forward.

Clown 1 pushed her into a bathroom.

Zoe threw out her hands and grabbed the edge of the basin to keep from falling. "You guys are quite the gentlemen, you know that?" She pivoted and closed the door.

He moved his foot forward.

The door bounced back and hit Zoe in the forehead. "Son-of-a," she held her head, finishing the muffled curse under the blanket. Rubbing the tender spot, she glared at him. "How about some privacy?"

He never budged.

She sidestepped toward the toilet. "Is this how you get your jollies?"

His eyes wandered down and up her body before he

turned ninety degrees, crossed arms over his chest, put his back to the doorjamb and looked straight ahead.

Gaping at the side of his face, Zoe threw off the covering and sat; the brown, padded plastic seat whooshed under her bodyweight. "You damn well better leave a quarter on the counter...because this isn't a freebie." She watched his shoulders rock up and down a few times and heard muted laughter. "Yeah, this is real funny."

With an audible backdrop of a liquid stream hitting porcelain, Zoe glanced around the room and saw only the bare necessities. The labels on the shower toiletries were outdated. A new bar of soap and a roll of paper towels rested on the vanity. The peeling paint on the walls was an ugly shade of orange she had never before seen. At her feet, between her and the shower, was an open magazine, showing more of another woman's body than Zoe cared to see.

Turning away from the image of the naked girl, she reached for the toilet paper, finished and stood. After washing and drying her hands, she was led back to her cell. The door closed and locked behind her. She faced Ayda. "I think we're in the woods somewhere...maybe Upstate New York."

"What makes you say that?"

"I got a peek outside. It was dark, but I could see trees...a lot of them. Plus, everything in the bathroom was...*old*...like it's been a long time since anyone actually *lived* here. We might be in a cabin."

"Well it's not like we can do anything about it. We're prisoners."

Zoe sat beside her sister, who had a similar blanket around her body. "You never know. We need to keep our eyes and ears open, in case we get a chance. If that happens, we need to jump on it."

"Yeah..." Ayda motioned toward Zoe's backside, her mind envisioning the cut beneath the green fabric, "and how'd that work out for you last time?"

Zoe shook her head. "Doesn't matter. Never give up."

Ayda regarded her sibling out of a half-closed eye. "When did you get so headstrong and determined?"

Zoe swiveled on her butt and reclined, fluffing the pillow under her head. "I've always been like this, Ay. Only you've never seen it. Or should I say *acknowledged* it?"

Ayda claimed her half of the narrow bed and stared at the ceiling. Her mind took her back to all the times Zoe had talked her down from an asthma attack, or led the way into some unknown adventure, or just sat with her and listened, as she poured out her heart. Ayda looked around the room. *Or kept me grounded in a crisis.*

Zoe rolled to her left shoulder, "You really don't have to mother me anymore, Ay," before she turned the other way, trying to ease her discomfort. "Just because I like to have fun doesn't—" making a face, she shuddered and drew in a short breath, "doesn't mean I don't have a brain."

Ayda fumbled with her blanket before finding and holding her sister's hand. "I think I'm starting to learn that." She squeezed. "I'm sorry. I'll try to do better in the future. I promise."

Feeling the sensation of a thousand needles poking her back, Zoe gripped Ayda's hand tighter. "Thanks," she grunted, while trying to find a comfortable position. "I'm going to hold you to that promise."

8:16 P.M.
NEW YORK CITY
MIDTOWN MANHATTAN

Jacob found a parking spot on 43rd Street, near Second Avenue. He ran the gearshift to 'P' and shut off the Ford's engine. Having handed off Paul Gentry to arriving FBI agents, and arranged for someone to drive Mrs. Gentry back to her house, Jacob and Stockwell had time to kill. Mr. Gentry was to drop off the ransom money at ten o'clock this evening. With no new leads from Higs to follow, they would be participating in the money drop.

Stockwell unhooked her seatbelt, opened the door and put one shoe on the running board. She looked over her shoulder. "You coming?"

He rested hands on his thighs, glanced out his window before looking through the windshield. A moment later, he made eye contact with her.

She spun back around and shut her door. "What's bothering you?" In the faint beam from the dome light, she had noticed a look in his eyes, a look she had seen earlier, one of sadness, emptiness. "What's wrong, Jake?"

He gave her a weak smile. "It's nothing. I'm fine. Let's go eat." He rotated his shoulders and grasped the door handle.

She clutched his upper arm.

He pivoted her way.

"No, you're not."

His lips disappearing inside his mouth, Jacob ogled her. "We've already discussed this. I don't want to bring it up again."

"Well, whatever it is, it's obviously still troubling you, so..." rocking onto her left hip, Stockwell crossed her right leg over her left, pulled her skirt's hem down a bit and leaned on the center console, her focus never straying from him, "we're not going anywhere, until you talk to me."

Turning away, he filled his lungs, and bit his lower lip for a few seconds before studying her again. "Persistent, aren't you?"

She nodded once. "Yes, I am."

"All right," he cleared his throat, "this assignment...Ayda and Zoe," he bobbed his head to the right, "and the previous one—the two little kids...and Samantha Chen and Felicity McNeil," he paused, "they all just remind me of—" his voice caught and he clamped shut his mouth. He tipped his head down and drew a breath through his nostrils.

Stockwell recognized the names, except for the last one; they were all people she and Jacob had saved from kidnappers or assassins. Remaining quiet, giving him time to compose himself, his thoughts, she glanced through the windshield.

The streets of New York City were alive, cars moving about, people hustling to their next destination. Moments earlier, when her door was open, she had caught a whiff of steak from a nearby restaurant. Now her stomach was telling her she wanted beef instead of pizza.

"Sometimes I..." Jacob grimaced, "I just can't shake the feeling that...that D.D. is going through the same thing...alone somewhere, wondering if anyone is coming to get her...namely *me*."

Stockwell faced him. She saw his cheek muscles contracting every other second.

He blew out a quick breath. "That's if she's even still alive."

"Jake," she snatched his hand, "your daughter's..." Stockwell stopped speaking, her mouth hanging open, her mind going through a dozen things to say. She regarded him. *He's right. His daughter could be dead, or she could be alive and waiting for him. Or there could be any number of other possible scenarios between the two.* Her gaze settled on the hand she held. *Just comfort him, Dee.*

Her chest falling, she exhaled a big breath and lifted her eyes. "Jake, I know that seeing these people, these innocent people, in similar situations to your D.D., must bring up awful feelings." She fumbled, half thinking of her next words, half praying for inspiration. "You...you can't let it get to you though. I realize that may seem empty, coming from someone who has no idea what you're going through, but...but..." she pivoted her head and shut her eyes. *Come Holy Spirit. Give me Your words.* She beheld Jacob. "You have to have faith, Jake."

He looked her way.

Her palms came together, sandwiching his hand between them. "What is it you tell the grieving relatives of those who are missing...or taken? Don't you ask them to put their faith," she pointed, "in *you*? I didn't hear what you told Mrs. Gentry back at her house, but I can only imagine it was something similar."

In his mind, Jacob recalled the scene she was referring to, as he stared through the windshield...

> *Jacob blinked a few times and swallowed. "What I'm trying to tell you is, to me...your daughters are not just another missing person's case." He paused. "I promise you. I'm going to do everything in my power to find Ayda and Zoe. You just have to have a little faith, ma'am."*

"Jake, until we have evidence to the contrary, D.D. is still alive. *And...*you and I are going to find her."

With the world racing by outside the F-150, stillness consumed the vehicle's interior for more than half a minute. During the intermittent moments when the surrounding commotion subsided, Stockwell's long, slow breaths could be heard.

Jacob nodded and kissed the back of her hand. "Thank you."

"You're welcome."

"You know…" he observed her in the ambient light from the street lamps, "you're pretty good at this faith and hope stuff."

"Like I've said before…you don't spend twelve years in parochial school and not learn a thing or two." Pausing, Stockwell focused her attention on the dashboard, thinking of her quick prayer a minute ago. She shot out a quick puff of air. "I guess it's all coming back to me again."

After admiring her for several moments, he lifted a corner of his mouth. "I'm lucky to have you, Deanna."

Facing him, she grinned. "Luck had nothing to do with it."

He frowned.

"As soon as I decided I wanted you," she snapped her fingers, "you were mine. Nothing you could've done."

Jacob leaned away, his eyebrows high. "Is that so?"

"Yup. Just like in the wild, the female attracts the male." Half-closing one eye at him, "Sooner or later," she barely nodded her head, "I knew you'd come knocking at my door."

Jacob flashed a grin.

She paired his mischievous smile with her last words. "I don't mean *that* door—well not right away anyway. I mean, *yeah…eventually*, but," she waved a hand between them, "knocking on my *apartment* door, okay?"

He laughed. "I knew what you meant from the

beginning, Stockwell. I was there remember, *with* pizza?"

Her eyes grew bigger. "Speaking of pizza," letting go of his hand, she gripped the door handle, "I'm starving. Can we go eat now?"

. . .

Jacob and Stockwell had lucked out and gotten a combination booth-and-chair table in the crowded, noisy restaurant. He had taken the booth side, his back to the windows, horizontal blinds drawn. At his nine o'clock was a short wall, a server's station on the other side.

"Okay," their server, a woman in her twenties with short blonde hair, "here we..." slid an elevated, silver-colored tray between two plates in the center of the square table, "go...one meat-lover's pizza with extra cheese and extra bacon."

Resting on the table, Stockwell's phone vibrated.

The server aimed index fingers at her patron's half-full drinking glasses. "Do you need refills?"

Jacob waved a hand. "I'm good."

Stockwell tapped the screen on her mobile, "No, thank you," and put the device to her ear. "Special Agent Stockwell."

Upon hearing the familiar term, the server cranked her head toward the female FBI agent before eyeing Jacob. "Are you two cops?"

He put his index finger to puckered lips and smiled. "We're keeping a low profile."

Stockwell's voice went deeper, louder. "What time?"

Jacob flicked his eyes toward his partner.

"What's the new location?"

The server smiled back at him. "Well," her voice quieter, "just let me know if I can get you anything else."

Stockwell nodded. "Okay, we're on our way."

Lifting a finger, "Hold on..." Jacob glimpsed a name on a small square napkin on the table, "Jessica," before facing his partner. "What is it, Stockwell?"

She ended the call and stood. "The kidnappers changed the drop-off location. Agents are scrambling to get into position as we speak." She faced the server. "We need the check please."

Rising to his feet, "Don't bother," Jacob fished out a hundred-dollar bill and surrendered the note to Jessica. "This should cover it." He quickly wrapped four slices of pizza in a thick cloth doily and plucked his jacket from the back of a chair. He raised the expensive makeshift food container a little higher. "You mind if we take this napkin?"

The woman shot a look at the money in her hand and came back to him. "I think you could take a few more if you wanted to."

He chuckled on his way by her. "One's enough. Thank you."

     ABOVE & BEYOND

10:05 P.M.
LOWER MANHATTAN
RAZOR'S EDGE NIGHT CLUB

Multi-colored lights flashed from different parts of the large room. A thumping bass beat blasted from six-foot speakers on the upper-level stage, and from smaller ones around the outside walls. Originating from near the DJ's feet, a light haze of smoke wafted upward before hanging over the crowded dance floor.

As the mix master, dressed in leather, gold chains and black sunglasses, the bill of his hat cocked to one side, bobbed his head and shoulders to the rhythm, the throng of twenty and thirty-something dancers—men acting tough, women wearing little clothing—gyrated to the music and bumped into each other every few seconds.

Low tables, high tables, couches, chairs and stools were strategically situated inside the club to give partyers a place to rest, and to refuel for the next song.

Paul Gentry sat on a wooden stool at one of those stations, a high table, near the middle of the dance floor. His back was to a white Roman column that rose to the ceiling. His hands rested on a black bowling bag on his lap. Once the kidnappers received the ransom, Gentry would get a text message, telling him where to find Ayda and Zoe.

With drinks in hand, their backs pressed against the edge of the bar, Jacob and Stockwell sat on padded stools, thirty feet from the man with the money. They nursed the beverages, only wetting their lips from time to time. Tipping his head from one side to the other, trying to keep Gentry in sight, Jacob glimpsed her out of the corner of his eye. "This plan sucks, Stockwell. You know that, right?"

She shot him a look and casually sliced fingers across her throat.

Both of them wore ear buds, and were on the same channel as the FBI agents posted throughout the establishment, including Carter Williams, the man in charge of the operation.

"I don't care who hears me." Jacob pivoted his head and stared through the swaying arms, toward Williams' position in the club. "Carter, this plan sucks. You know as well as I do that when the kidnappers get the money, the hostages lose their value...and become liabilities."

Stockwell squeezed her teammate's arm. "Jake."

Through the communication channel, Agent Williams: "You've made your concerns well known, Jake. And maybe they'd carry more weight *if* you were still with the bureau. You're here as a courtesy only. Remember that."

Jacob came back to Stockwell, shaking his head at

her, while peering at Gentry beyond her right shoulder.

The music dropped a bit.

Gentry: "I just got a text message. They want me to leave the bag and walk away. What do I do?"

The DJ's voice: "By special request, here's a tune you'll all know."

"This is Agent Williams. Follow their instructions. Get up and walk away. We've got eyes on the prize."

Jacob rolled his eyes at Williams' last words. *Who says that anymore?*

DJ: "Everybody on yo' feet...and shake it to the beat."

The music jumped to a new level of loudness.

Gentry stood, put the bowling bag on his stool and pushed his way through the horde of young people.

Recognizing the song, every person in the club rushed to the dance floor. Shoulder-to-shoulder, hip-to-hip, people only had enough room to wave their arms over their heads.

Losing sight of Gentry, and the black bag, Jacob sat erect before sliding off the stool. "I don't have a visual anymore."

Several FBI agents echoed similar comments.

Jacob glanced at the dancers and twirled a finger in the air. "This," he shouted, "is what they wanted. The kidnappers called in that request. They're making their move." He pushed people left and right, forcing his way forward, toward Gentry's table. "All agents," he shoved a man, "cover the exits. I'm going for the drop-off point."

Stockwell followed in his wake.

He separated himself from the masses, looked in all directions, stooped and scanned the area under the table. "The money's gone."

She bumped into him from behind.

After whipping his head back and forth, Jacob climbed onto the high table and did a couple of three-sixty's.

Stockwell looked up at him, while covering the ear with no communication device in it. "Does anyone have eyes on the money bag?"

Several choruses of 'Negative' came back to her.

Jacob stopped and slanted right to see around the Roman column. He squinted at a green, Army-style jacket. The man wearing the garment was not dancing. He was snaking through the people. The man turned sideways, and Jacob saw the black bag. "I got him." Knowing the front door was behind him, he rotated his head left, toward the back door. "He's not heading for an exit."

Agent Williams: "Give me his position."

Jacob jumped off the table. "Stockwell, stay behind me." He lifted his arms in front of his body and drove ahead, full steam.

She slipped eight fingers inside the waistband of his pants and hunched forward.

Williams: "Damn it, St. Christopher. Give me a position. Where is the target heading?"

Jacob slid a metal scissor gate to the left and ran down a short hallway.

Stockwell followed.

He turned right; a long and narrow hall, with curtain-covered archways on either side, lay ahead. With the deafening music fading behind him, he fast walked to the first black covering on the right and threw open the thick sheet.

At the sound of a metal ring scraping across a metal bar, a woman—her bare back to the agents—stopped bouncing up and down on a rickety, creaking mattress. Both she and the man under her looked toward the gawkers.

Jacob let go of the sheet and hurried down the hall, pointing. "You take the left side."

Stockwell cleared her rooms, witnessing acts she had only ever heard about, and met him outside the last sex den on the right.

He met her gaze. "You see anything?"

She slammed shut her eyes, "Only that which I," before blinking several times and shaking her head, "hope to one day be able to forget."

"Let's keep going." Jacob bolted down the hallway that only veered to the left. He took the turn and came face-to-face with a beefy man in jeans, wearing a leather vest over his hairy chest.

"This," Beefy grabbed Jacob, "is a restricted area. You

aren't allow—"

Thrusting his arms upward, between Beefy's forearms, Jacob broke the hold. He clutched Beefy's head with both hands, wrenched downward and drove a knee into the man's nose.

Enfolding his gushing nose, Beefy crashed back against the wall, slid to his butt and listed sideways.

Jacob ran, Stockwell on his heels.

A woman with purple-colored, spiked hair, the same height as him, repeated the same 'restricted area' speech as Beefy, while inserting several foul words. She cocked her right arm.

"She's yours, Stockwell." Jacob ducked under the blow, redirected the right cross into the concrete wall to his right and kept going, never losing a step.

Swerving left, but not stopping, Stockwell landed a right elbow to Purple's exposed rib cage.

The woman grabbed her side.

Pivoting right, Stockwell connected with a left cross to Purple's right cheek.

The woman fell to all fours before sprawling onto the floor.

Stockwell continued running, several paces behind her fellow agent.

After taking a right turn at the next junction, Jacob crashed through a door, into the open night air. Tall buildings around him blocked the moonlight. A few distant streetlights provided minimal illumination. He jogged forward, the soles of his boots connecting with a metal grating. He grabbed a handrail in front of him, inclined forward and scanned the dark alley below.

Stockwell exited the building before the door could shut. She stopped on his right, surveying the street scene with him. Her chest swelled. "There was a *third* exit." She exhaled. "We missed it."

Both agents were breathing heavily, as they listened, hoping to catch the sound of their quarry: a scuffing shoe, a stomping boot, a splashing puddle.

Jacob looked left, down an alley that led to a busy street; cars crisscrossed under a traffic light. Pedestrians walked parallel with the cars and trucks.

The agents faced straight ahead when lights flashed and a horn beeped twice.

A door opened and closed. An engine started. Headlights came on and the vehicle lurched forward, toward Jacob and Stockwell.

Jacob darted to his left, "That has to be him," along the metal walkway. "There's nowhere else he could've gone." Coming to the end of the walkway, he climbed over the handrail.

The headlights grew brighter before changing directions and lighting up the alley that led to the congested street.

Holding the bar behind his back, his heels clinging to the lip of the walkway, Jacob gave the turning vehicle a last look and leaped forward.

"Jake!" Stockwell's thighs hit the handrail, as she reached for her man.

He dropped onto a low, angled awning, slid a short ways to the right on the smooth metal, caught his balance, and raced forward.

The vehicle accelerated.

Hearing the engine rev, stealing glimpses at the Chevrolet S10-shaped truck, at his three o'clock and almost ten feet below him, Jacob kept pace with the escaping pickup. His eyes flicked back and forth—the truck, the awning...truck, awning.

Reaching the end of the corrugated footpath, he drove off his left foot, threw out his arms and jumped. Flying through the air, he heard Stockwell's shriek.

"Jake!"

Landing feet first in the bed of the truck, Jacob rolled onto his right hip before he collided with the wheel well, smacking his shoulder blade on the sheet metal. He grimaced, while his momentum carried him over the side of the pickup. He reached for a solid purchase. His middle finger found one of the tie-down loops and he pulled his body back inside.

The man in the Army jacket yanked the steering wheel left and right.

Jacob was thrown backward before he was propelled forward, further into the bed. He crawled to the sliding glass window and rose to his knees. Meeting the kidnapper's gaze in the rearview mirror, he reached inside his leather jacket.

Army did another left/right maneuver.

His knees and feet spread wide, Jacob countered the motions and stayed in place. A moment later, he smashed the glass with the 357 Coonan.

Army tapped the brake pedal, throwing his passenger into the two-person cab.

Jacob stopped when his thighs hit the outside of the truck. On his belly, half inside and half outside the speeding vehicle, he lifted the 1911. "Stop the—"

Army grabbed the gun's slide, and a forty-mile-per-hour grappling match ensued.

Jacob threw two left elbows into the man's face.

His shoulder hitting the door, the man pulled the steering wheel to the left. The S10 lurched in the same direction, careening along the backs of buildings, leaving behind a trail of sparks.

Army returned the truck to the center of the alley, while continuing the tug-of-war for the gun.

Jacob stole a peek out the front window. They were nearing the street. Shoving the side of his opponent's face into the left window, Jacob flexed his right bicep and slowly brought the Magnum toward the kidnapper.

Army pushed back.

After spying the speedometer—forty-five miles per hour—Jacob looked ahead. More than two dozen pedestrians were quickly approaching.

Resisting Jacob's force, the driver stretched out his right foot, flattening the gas pedal against the floor.

Jacob whipped his head toward Army before gaping at the walkers. *They'll be massacred.* He came back to the driver, to his only lead on finding Ayda and Zoe. *I need him alive.*

The S10 zoomed forward, reaching fifty miles per hour.

Jacob glimpsed the foot-travelers—talking, laughing, noses pressed against cell phones. They were unaware of their fate.

Fifty-five miles per hour...

He gritted his teeth. *Damn it.* Curling his left arm

around Army's neck, Jacob brought the man's head closer, while forcing the 357's muzzle toward his adversary's chest.

Still grasping the Coonan, Army pushed, but the big hole at the end of the barrel turned his way.

Fifty-seven miles per hour...

Turning his face away from the forthcoming blast, Jacob cast a quick glance toward the cross street, and pressed the trigger.

The pistol roared, the report somewhat muffled by the green Army jacket. The 158-grain jacketed hollow-point bullet left the barrel and expanded on impact, creating a devastating wound channel.

Army's heart exploded, his body seizing before going limp.

Jacob crawled to the floorboard, yanked the dead man's foot off the accelerator and jammed the brake pedal forward.

The older Chevy's brakes squealed. The tires screeched over the pavement.

The sudden change in velocity threw Jacob closer to the foot controls, the right side of his face mashing against the vertical bar attached to the brake pedal. His legs were thrown into the cab.

The truck fishtailed left. Its left-rear quarter panel clipped a dumpster, and the lightweight vehicle briefly went up on two wheels before spinning around once and stopping.

Jacob's eyes zipped in all directions, as the S10 rocked a couple times and settled. Hearing the motor idling on the other side of the firewall, near his head, he pushed up on the gearshift and turned the ignition switch; the engine stopped running. His body contorted into an awkward pose, he thought back to his teenage years when he had to get into similar positions to replace hard-to-reach parts on his older cars. He bobbed his eyebrows once. *Haven't done this in a while.*

He kicked the passenger door open, wriggled out from under the steering wheel and backed out of the truck. Standing erect, he straightened his jacket, and rolled his shoulders and neck, loosening muscles.

Out of the corner of his eye, he spotted a group of young women, dressed in clubbing attire—high heels and not much else—gathering around him. He nodded at them, "Ladies," before racking the slide on the Coonan, clearing the malfunction and chambering a fresh round.

Their faces paling, the women backed away.

"It's all right." He raised a hand. "I'm with Homeland Security." He holstered the weapon and showed his badge. "Is everyone okay? Did anyone get hurt?" After receiving negative replies, he gaped at the corpse behind the wheel and shook his head. *Son...of...a...* in his peripheral vision, he saw a figure running full tilt toward him.

The woman skidded to a halt and clutched his shoulders before inspecting his frame. Her forehead displayed horizontal squiggly lines, while her chest heaved, as she took huge gulps of air.

"I'm fine, Stockwell. No bullet holes. No broken bones." He faced the dead man. "But our only lead on finding the girls...wasn't as fortunate."

Catching her breath, she joined him in staring at the truck's dead driver.

Several seconds passed.

Jacob eyed the growing crowd.

In the distance, approaching emergency vehicles could be heard.

He rotated his head toward her. "We need to—"

She made a fist and slugged him.

Grabbing his arm, "Ow!" he glimpsed the spot she had hit and frowned at her. "Why'd you hit me?"

She leveled a finger at him. "You know why. I'm thirty-one." Her voice grew louder. "Thirty-one-year-olds are *not* supposed to have heart attacks."

Standing in a semi-circle around the spatting couple, the gawking women gave one another looks.

Jacob rubbed the sore muscle.

"When I saw you jump off that roof..." Stockwell shut her eyes and turned away before coming back at full force, "and then I saw you half hanging," she gestured at the truck, "out of *this* thing." She clutched his jacket's lapels, on either side of his chin and pulled him down to her height. "I...you...I..." she let out a heavy sigh, pitched forward and squashed his lips with hers.

The onlookers grinned.

Stockwell pulled away, but kept her mouth close to his. "I thought I was going to have a heart attack, Jake. Please tell me you won't do something like that again."

He half smiled. "I can *tell you that*, but..."

Her eyes zipped across every square inch of his face. "...I can't—"

"Make any promises...I get it."

"You of all people, Stockwell, should know the danger we face every day."

She slowly nodded. "I do. It comes with the job."

The faraway sirens were closer, louder.

His hands curved around to her lower back. "I *can* promise you this...I love you."

Letting out a low groan, she took his head in both hands and gently jostled him. "I love you too," she flashed a smile, "you crazy man you."

The wailing alarms were almost on top of them.

After a short snigger, Jacob patted her back and pecked her cheek. "Come on." He eyed the police cars, strobe lights flashing, coming to a halt where the alley met the cross street. "We need to see if Higs has made any progress on locating that van."

10:29 P.M.

"He's dead, Higs. I had no choice." Jacob put the phone on the console. "If I didn't do something, a lot of people were going to get hurt." After a verbal confrontation with Agent Williams, over Jacob's pursuit of the kidnapper, and the man's resultant death, Jacob and Stockwell walked away from a seething Williams and made their way back to the F-150. "I couldn't let that happen."

"I understand, Mr. St. Christopher."

Stockwell attached her seatbelt and observed the mobile. "Are we any closer to finding that van, Higs?"

"Based on all of the available data I've uploaded into my algorithms, including video footage of a black van matching the description of the one we're seeking..."

Jacob and Stockwell heard Higs take an audible breath and exhale.

"...I've come up with several possible locations where the kidnappers could have taken Ayda and Zoe."

Jacob started the Ford. "Several won't cut it, Higs. We need *one*. Once the other kidnappers figure out the money drop didn't happen, they're going to panic and start tying up loose ends."

"I understand the ramifications, Mr. St. Christopher."

"Then tell us where we need to be."

"There are more than a dozen properties that are loosely connected to Calvin Cole. All of which are in Upstate New York. You, and Ms. Stockwell, cannot possibly search every one of them. I'm uploading the new data on the man you—"

"Upstate New York." Jacob put the vehicle in gear, checked the side-view mirror and zipped into traffic. "That's a start. We're leaving the city now. Call when you have the list narrowed down."

"I should have something for you within the hour."

Jacob mashed the 'end' button. Minutes later, he spun the steering wheel, entered the on-ramp to I-87 and pressed the accelerator to the floorboard. The tires squealed before gaining traction.

. . .

11:31 P.M.
INTERSTATE 287
NEAR WEST NYACK, NEW YORK

Jacob's phone rang, an hour after he ended the last call from his boss. He tapped the screen. "Go ahead, Higs. We're here."

"I have narrowed the dozen possible locations down to the four most probable."

Jacob sighed and rolled his eyes toward Stockwell.

She ran an index finger back and forth between him and her. "We could split up, each of us taking two."

He wrinkled his nose. "We don't know what kind of

enemy contingent we'd be running into...we need to stay together."

"I can call Williams and see if he'll send teams to the other three sites."

"We're not exactly in his good graces at the moment." A beat. "And what would we say to convince him...some smart computer guy—who we can't tell you his name— thinks the girls are at one of these four places? He can't commit resources based on that evidence." Jacob glanced at the mobile. "What's on those four properties, Higs?"

"Three of them are residential homes in small-to-medium-sized towns."

"And the fourth?"

"The fourth property is a large swath of wooded, undeveloped land with a small, old home set back from the road. I'm unsure if anyone is currently residing on the premises. Electrical usage has been minimal over the last twelve months. Substantial upticks in late October through November; however, would seem to suggest the structure may be in use as a hunting cabin."

Jacob whipped his head toward the cell on the console. "Hunting cabin?" His mind took him back to the living room at Cole's home in Queens. He eyed Stockwell. "Those photos you took at Cole's place before we left...did you happen to get a shot of the mantle over the fireplace?"

She swiped her thumb over her phone's screen several times.

"She did indeed, Mr. St. Christopher. I utilized a specific photo on the mantle to tie Mr. Cole to an elderly man named," a pause, "Fred Johnston. He owns the hunting cabin in question."

"I got it." Stockwell showed Jacob the image.

Jacob pointed, "That picture," while going back to watching traffic, "on the mantle...all the way on the right...can you make it bigger?"

She spread her fingers over the screen, enlarging and centering the individual photo.

Jacob rotated his head back and forth, from her phone to the road ahead, examining the picture of a dead deer and three men—rifles in hand—posing with their kill. "Higs, is Fred Johnston in that shot?"

"Yes. He's the one on the left. Mr. Cole's late grandfather is the gentleman on the other side of Cole. Calvin Cole's father died when Calvin was a baby."

Jacob wagged his finger at Stockwell's mobile device. "That's where they took Ayda and Zoe."

"Jake," Stockwell gestured at her cell, "that picture could've been taken anywhere. What makes you think—"

"Hold on." He took her phone. Flicking his eyes left and right, he kept track of cars ahead, while zeroing in on the screen. "There's something on a tree...in the upper right corner, on the edge of the photo...just beyond Grandfather Cole's shoulder." He forfeited the cell. "What's that look like to you?"

She made the image as big as she could and

scrutinized the blurry shape on the tree. A second later, she squinted before her eyes grew bigger. "That's a survey marker."

Jacob smiled and nodded at her. "Higs..."

"I've already cleaned up the image, and it is indeed a survey marker. I'm running a search as we speak. Give me a minute."

She faced Jacob. "What are you thinking?"

"I'm thinking," he checked mirrors, changed lanes and passed a car, "if that marker is from Fred Johnston's property, then we have another link...back to Cole taking Ayda and Zoe to," he dipped his forehead toward her mobile, "*that* location. Think about it, Stockwell. It's secluded. He knows the area. He's comfortable there. It's a perfect place to hide two young women."

Stockwell nodded. "You're right. That's what I would do." She glanced his way. "If I was a psychotic kidnapper, that is."

Higs: "That survey marker is in fact located on Mr. Fred Johnston's property."

"Send the address to Stockwell's phone, Higs."

"Done. What is your current location?"

"We're on 287, coming up on the exit for West Nyack."

"Stay on Interstate 287. You...are...twenty minutes away. You should arrive by midnight."

11:53 P.M.

Five-ten, one-seventy, muscular build, the late-twenties Calvin Cole groomed his goatee with his fingers, while staring at the throwaway cell phone in his other hand.

"Something went wrong. He should've called by now, *been here* by now."

Seated on a couch in the cabin's main living space, legs crossed—ankle on knee—Cole lifted his gaze toward his right-hand man, his most trusted friend. "Settle down, Pete."

"I'm telling you." Pacing back and forth over a bearskin rug, Pete—the same height as Cole, but twenty pounds lighter—waved his arms before taking a long drag on a cigarette and jamming a finger at Cole. "Something went wrong. He's not coming. The cops got him. Hell, for all we know he could've just taken the money and left town."

Cole's eyes dropped. The man he had sent to pick up the ransom was almost as trustworthy as Pete was. Cole studied the phone again. *Anyone can get greedy I suppose.*

Pete made another trip over the bear's fur. "We need to get out of here. If the cops have him...and he told them where we are..."

Cole washed a hand down his face, crossed his arms and looked away, in the direction of the room holding his prisoners. *They still haven't seen our faces. They don't know who we are. We can just up and leave. They won't be able to ID us.*

"Vinny, this whole damn thing's been screwed up from the beginning. I told you. We should have never demanded more money. We got greedy." Pete made another back and forth. "It's going to cost us. I'm telling you. It's going to cost us."

Cole squinted at the wall separating him and Pete from the two women in their custody. *Can't argue with that...and who's to say someone didn't slip-up and talk to the girls, or show them his face?*

"We need to cut our losses." Pete stopped in front of his friend. "We need to cut them and run, Vinny."

Cole half closed an eye at the standing man before glimpsing the wall, his mind seeing the women. *I agree.* He stood. "Tell the other two to load up the van. And then," he poked Pete's chest, "meet me out back at the shed."

"What are we going to do?"

Cole left the living room. "Take care of a couple loose ends."

. . .

11:55 P.M.

Hearing the lock turn and seeing the door open, Ayda and Zoe sat up in bed.

Cole entered the room. "Get up. Let's go."

Zoe's cheeks blanched. Her heart rate spiked. Her stomach twisted into a thousand tiny knots. This was the first time she had seen any of the kidnapper's faces. Now she, and her sister, could identify one of them.

Ayda stared at Zoe.

"I said," Cole charged across the room, grabbed Ayda by the arm, "*get,*" and flung her toward the door, "*up.*"

Zoe leaped from the mattress.

He sent her reeling with a backhand to the side of her face.

Ayda stepped toward him.

Cole drew a Smith & Wesson M&P9 from the back of his waistband and aimed the gun at her.

Ayda stopped.

He swung the pistol toward Zoe. "No more of your games," he leaned heavy on his next words, "Zo Zo."

She rubbed her stinging cheek.

"Now *get...up.*" He waved the Smith toward the door. "We're going to take a walk outside. I hear it's a nice night for a stroll."

JULY 25TH; 12:01 A.M.
NORTH OF SLOATSBURG, NEW YORK

Halfway up the two-hundred-yard dirt driveway, lined with tall trees on either side, Jacob parked the F-150 sideways between two hulking oaks, one near each bumper, leaving no room for another vehicle to slip by the barricade.

Stockwell had her door open before the Ford stopped rolling.

He jumped out of the truck, while peeling off his shoulder holster. He swapped out his gray dress shirt for a black tactical one, adding a bulletproof vest underneath. After gathering the gear he would need from the metal box, he hurried around to the passenger side. Spying Stockwell—her back to him, bent over, barefoot and stepping out of her skirt—Jacob lost a step when he spotted her white, lace women's boy shorts.

She stood erect, her white tank top sliding down to meet the underwear's elastic waistband.

Jacob regained his composure and drew up behind her. "I see there's a full moon out tonight."

Stockwell tossed the skirt and lifted an eyebrow at him.

ALEX ANDER   177

Hearing his words again, he quickly pointed skyward. "Up there."

A half smile on her face, she put on her lightweight bulletproof vest.

Jacob wrestled into his shoulder holster again. "That won't matter when we're in the trees, but," he added a tactical vest, "it'll make us easier to spot in open spaces."

She added a black, long-sleeved, button-up shirt, black tactical pants and black, six-inch side-zip boots, all from 5.11 Tactical, before securing her hair in a mid-rise ponytail. "We'll stick to the trees on approach."

"That's what I thought too." He held up her tactical vest.

She pivoted.

He slid the garment over her shoulders and grabbed a sound-suppressed nine-millimeter Heckler & Koch MP5 from the metal box. "Your usual?"

She zipped the vest and took the rifle from him. "Have we really been together that long that you already know my *usual* weapon of choice?"

Handing over additional 30-round curved magazines, "You bring stealth and..." Jacob grinned and picked up his Mossberg 590 Shockwave SPX; a 12-gauge, 26-inch shotgun with 14-inch, heavy-walled breaching barrel, "I bring the boom."

Stockwell slung her MP5 around her neck and smiled. "I guess they're right...opposites do attract."

Using a special attachment, he slung the short

shotgun from his shoulder harness, below the spare 1911 magazines under his right armpit. "You ready?" He finessed a communication device into his ear.

After verifying the status of her Glock 19M and sliding the weapon into the front-mounted horizontal holster on her vest, she inserted an ear bud, clutched the MP5 and nodded. "Ready."

. . .

12:06 A.M.

Barefoot, a gun pointed at their backs—Ayda in a skirt and blouse; Zoe wearing a skirt, and naked from the waist up—the women plodded forward. They stumbled into divots and tripped over small rocks and tree limbs.

Her breathing becoming more erratic, Ayda leaned closer to her younger sibling. "This feels," she grabbed a short breath, "bad."

Hearing the hitch in her sister's voice, Zoe faced Ayda. "Stay calm, Ay. Don't give up on me now. In through the nose and out through the mouth, slow and steady. Let me handle the rest."

Cole pushed Zoe. "Shut up and move."

Zoe tumbled and landed on her hands and knees.

He grabbed a handful of her hair, hoisted her to her feet and shoved again. "Hurry up." After the women entered a small grove of trees, he stole a glance over his shoulder, spying the black van, and his men loading the vehicle. A second later, he disappeared into the forest.

12:08 A.M.

Down on one knee, a few feet inside the tree line, each with an ATN NVM14-4 monocular held to one eye, Jacob and Stockwell scanned a cabin—fifty yards away—and the structure's perimeter.

Two people stood near a van, backed up to the right corner of the front porch. One of the men slammed shut the rear door, while the other lit a cigarette. Both turned their backs on the hidden spectators and stared into the distance.

Jacob aimed his night vision device in the same direction the men were gawking. He saw nothing. "Thoughts?" he whispered.

Stockwell kept her voice low. "They're waiting for something."

"Or some*one*. Let's take them, while they're in the open." Looking left, he swung his left arm outward. "Stay in the trees and come in from the left. I'll use the van for concealment and—"

"Too late."

He faced forward.

Both men headed for the cabin, one stomping out his ciggy on the dirt driveway. They walked into the house and closed the door.

On his right, Stockwell pivoted her head toward him. "Now what?"

"Now I get to," using his elbow, he pressed the

Mossberg to his rib cage, "bring the hammer." He peered through the monocular, focusing on the doorknob. "I don't see a deadbolt, so we'll enter after I blow the latch on the first shot."

"Copy that."

"You go lef—"

"I'll go left and low," she interrupted. "You take high and right."

He smiled. "We know each other so well."

"Opposites may attract, but," she crouched and checked her equipment, "being on the same page...keeps you together."

"Amen to that." He stowed the monocular and clutched the Mossberg. "From now on...hand signals only, until we breach."

"Copy that. Going silent."

. . .

12:10 A.M.

Stopping at the right rear corner of the van, Jacob squatted and held up his left fist.

Behind him, Stockwell halted.

After a quick scan of the area, he chopped the air at his eleven o'clock.

In a low crouch, she hurried forward, up the porch steps, took a position on the left side of the door and pointed her MP5 at the knob on the right side.

A step behind her, Jacob squared off with the door, racked the 590 and put the muzzle against the space between the knob and the frame. He angled the shotgun forty-five degrees, down and in, and faced Stockwell.

She nodded.

He pressed the trigger.

The frangible breaching round splintered wood before disintegrating into powder.

He did a counter-clockwise one-eighty and donkey-kicked the door open.

Stockwell charged inside.

Jacob let go of the twelve-gauge, drew his 1911 and followed her.

She slid to the left.

He sidestepped right.

On the other side of the small cabin, a man lifted his right arm.

"FB—" spotting the firearm in his hand, she called out the last identification letter at the same time she pulled the trigger; a three-round burst left the MP5.

The man clutched the back of a couch with his free hand and let loose with two shots.

Stockwell flinched when two bullets zipped over her head and continued through the front window.

Jacob covered the gunman's nose with the Coonan's front sight, fired one round and swung the gun's muzzle back toward his half of the living room.

The gunman collapsed behind the couch.

Stockwell moved left.

Jacob moved right. After verifying the assailant was

neutralized, he met her at a short hallway.

A man exited a room, his pistol already pointed at the agents.

Jacob and Stockwell fired their weapons simultaneously; three nine-millimeter and two, 357 Magnum projectiles ended the threat.

They cleared three rooms. The last one had a bed, a lamp and a table. Power bars and plastic bottles were scattered on the table. Exchanging a partial magazine for a full one, he nodded at the food and water. "They were here."

"But where the hell are they now?"

He darted by her. "Out back...in the same direction those guys were staring."

. . .

ONE MINUTE EARLIER
12:09 A.M.

Ayda and Zoe emerged from the wooded area, Cole behind them. Made from unpainted boards, a small tool shed stood in the center of a clearing. The trio trudged toward the outbuilding.

"That's far enough."

The women stopped.

"What...are," Ayda drew a quick breath, "you going to do to us?"

Zoe wrapped her left arm around her struggling sister. "Take it easy. It's going to be okay."

"I want...to know..."

Pete appeared from the trees and approached the

threesome.

"...what...you're..."

Cole motioned with the gun. "Get the shovels from the shed."

Ayda gulped oxygen. "...going...to do."

Pete veered around the women and entered the shack. Twenty seconds later, he came out with a spade in each hand.

Ayda slowly filled her lungs. Breathing was a chore. "Oh my God," she cried. "No. No, you...can't do this." Her words were broken by short gasps for air. "Please. We won't," her chest swelled, "tell...anyone."

"What are we doing here, Vinny?"

"We're doing what needs to be done."

Pete held up the tools. "You never said anything about this. This was easy money you said; a quick score."

Ayda bent over at the waist. "Oh my God. No." Her upper body convulsing, *Dear God*, she sucked in her stomach, *please help us.*

Supporting more and more of her sister's weight, Zoe pivoted her head in all directions. Darkness was all around them. Her mind searched for a plan, a way out of the situation. She kept coming back to one. *Run and hope they don't find us.* Inwardly, she scoffed. *Or shoot us in the back. Some plan.*

"It *was* supposed to be easy money." Cole grabbed a shovel. "But *someone* just had to bring in his pals though, didn't he?"

Pete aimed the hand tool's pointed end at the other man. "You can't blame this on me. How was I—"

Coming from the direction of the cabin, gunshots pierced the calm night air.

Pete looked beyond his partner's shoulder.

Cole whipped his head around, toward the noise.

Grabbing the shovel, Zoe sent her foot into Cole's crotch and swung the gardening instrument at Pete. The bottom part of the spade glanced off the man's shoulder and hit the side of his face. "Run Ayda. Run!"

. . .

12:12 A.M.

They ran out of the cabin and raced toward the back of the property, Jacob covering right, Stockwell aiming her rifle left. Stopping, he crouched and raised his left fist.

Stockwell took a knee.

He dug out his ATN monocular from a vest pocket and viewed the area ahead.

She did the same before facing him. "What's the plan?"

"You come in from the left and flank him. I'm going up the gut."

"Copy that." She darted left.

Jacob hurried forward, drawing to within fifty feet of a man pointing a gun at a woman's right temple.

His belly to her back, his left arm around her stomach, left hand clutching her right breast, her other breast wedged in the crook of his arm, Pete backpedaled. "Stay away or I'll shoot her. I swear. I'll kill her. Get back."

Zoe kicked out her legs, scrambling to stay on her feet, as he dragged her alongside the shed. She flicked her eyes to the right and saw another figure.

On Jacob's ten o'clock, Stockwell closed the distance between her and the gunman, coming up on the man's right side.

Seeing Stockwell, Pete thrust out his weapon toward her. "I said get back," he jammed the muzzle into Zoe's head, "or I'll kill her." He aimed the pistol at Jacob, then Stockwell before pressing it against his captive's cheek. Pete cranked his head left and right, looking over both shoulders, as he backtracked toward the woods. "You hear me? I'll do it. I swear."

Doing his best to keep from aiming the Coonan at the hostage, Jacob advanced, matching Pete stride for stride. "Give it up. There's nowhere to go. It's over." He lowered his chin, "Stockwell," and his voice, "you got a shot?"

"It comes and goes," she whispered back.

As he backed away, Pete rotated his prisoner, using her as a shield.

"When you have it," Jacob growled, "take it. I'll open the angle."

"You sure about this?"

"I trust your aim." Passing the shack, Jacob

sidestepped to his right, forcing the assailant to expose more of his body to one agent or the other. "You can still walk away from this. No one has to die tonight."

Stockwell stopped moving.

"Don't be stupid." Jacob was careful not to get into a crossfire situation with his partner.

She set the MP5's selector switch to 'single shot' and acquired the target in her scope.

"You're young." Jacob crept to his right, increasing the distance between him and Stockwell. "You can still have a life."

She placed the red dot on Pete's ear when he pivoted away from her.

The hostage taker continued on his path toward the dense woods.

Zoe tugged on her captor's arm and pulled on the fingers pinching her nipple. Tears ran down her cheeks, as she was tossed about, staring down the muzzle of a pistol one moment and a rifle the next. Above the terror, she thought of Ayda. *Please God...please let her be all right.*

Jacob saw the kidnapper closing in on the trees, and the blackness beyond. "Can't," his voice was low and gruff, "let him get to the woods, Dee."

Stockwell flicked her eyes to the left, toward the tree line.

Jacob raised his voice. "Just let the woman go. I promise we won't hurt you."

Stockwell took a deep breath.

Pete and his human shield faced her.

Seeing the hostage's wet cheeks and bulging eyes in her scope, Stockwell let out half the air in her lungs, holding the rest.

Pete was a few paces from the woods.

Under his breath, Jacob: "Take him out, Stockwell." He raised his voice. "Over here, man. It's just you and me."

Closing her left eye, Stockwell touched the face of the MP5's trigger.

Pete turned toward the sound of Jacob's voice, taking Zoe with him.

Stockwell had a clear sight picture. The scope's red dot was exactly where she had left it. In one smooth motion, she eased back her right index finger.

The round-nose, 124-grain, nine-millimeter projectile entered Pete's ear and burrowed into his brain, shutting down all motor functions. His arms hung limp at his sides. His gun landed on the ground. His legs buckled and he dropped to his knees before his face pressed against the hostage's lower back.

Feeling freedom, Zoe ran.

Pete's body pitched forward and his lifeless face slammed into a thin bed of pine needles.

Zoe turned around. Crying, she covered her mouth with both hands, fell to her knees and sat on her ankles. Staring at the dead man's open eyes, she rolled onto her right hip. A split-second later, her upper body slanted in the same direction before falling.

Jacob lunged and caught her. "Make sure he *stays down*, Stockwell."

"I'm on it."

12:14 A.M.

Jacob bobbed his head backward, "...and this is Special Agent Stockwell," while sliding his arms back into his shoulder holster.

Stockwell smiled at the woman. "Call me Deanna."

Sitting on the ground, her upper body trembling, her fingers fumbling with a button on Jacob's shirt, Zoe lifted her head. "I'm Zoe." Lowering her chin to her chest, she went back to work. The shaking woman had yet to attach the first button.

Jacob reached out. "May I?"

She took a quick breath and let her hands fall to her lap. "Look at me. I can't even put on a shirt."

"That's to be expected, Miss Gentry...given the circumstances." Down on one knee in front of her, Jacob eyed his attire, covering the woman's bare chest. He fastened the second button down. "Where's Ayda?"

"I don't know. We heard a blast up by the," flinging her left arm outward, she batted his hand away from her body, "house. I'm sorry."

"That's okay." Doing every other one, Jacob attached the fourth button down.

"I told her to run. We got separated." Zoe shook her

head. "I don't know where she is. I think I saw her," she threw out her other arm, grazing Jacob's elbow, "run off into the woods."

He did button six. "Did anyone go after her?"

She nodded. "I think so. There were two men here. You killed one."

"How many men," her breasts still partially visible through a gap in the clothing, he fed button three into its hole, "did you see...in total?"

"I only ever saw," Zoe wrinkled her brow and looked away, "maybe," before facing him, "three at any one moment? They wore masks all the time...except at the end."

Standing, doing the math in his head, Jacob put on his tactical vest, over his black muscle shirt and protective vest. "Cole," he faced Stockwell, "must've gone after her."

"I think you're right. None of the others match his description."

"There could be more around here though. You stay with Zoe. I'm going after Ayda."

She nodded. "Be careful, Jake."

"You too."

He pivoted toward the trees.

Zoe leaped to her feet and seized his arm.

He cranked his head around and peered into watery eyes.

"Ayda has asthma."

He nodded. "We know."

"She was getting one of her attacks when this all started. You have to find her."

Feeling her nails cutting into his skin, Jacob gently peeled away her fingers and gave her a reassuring smile. "Trust me. I will." Rubbing the five, slightly curved indentations on his forearm, he headed for the tree line.

"You have to talk her down."

Jacob entered the forest.

Zoe went to tiptoes and raised her voice. "You need to tell her to focus on getting that first breath."

Cupping Zoe's shoulders, Stockwell got her attention. "I promise you." She tipped her head in Jacob's direction. "Jake will find your sister and take good care of her."

Biting her lower lip, Zoe shifted her eyes toward the woods, came back to Stockwell and slowly nodded her head.

Stockwell hugged the shorter woman.

Zoe hugged her back, squeezing as hard as she could.

A moment later, Stockwell recalled her words to the frightened woman: *I promise you.* Holding the back of Zoe's head, the FBI agent inwardly snorted and gazed toward the trees, toward her last image of Jacob. *I'm starting to sound like you now.*

· · ·

Stopping periodically to scan the area with his ATN monocular, Jacob had spent the last ten minutes searching the forest for Ayda. He came to the edge of a long, narrow lake. He looked across the water. In the moonlight, he could see the outlines of homes through gaps among the trees.

Putting the monocular to his eye, he panned right, along the lakeshore, before rotating his upper body and surveying the land to his left. He pulled the eyepiece away from his face, squinted at a mound near the tree line and looked through the glass again.

Stowing the ATN, he ran along the shoreline, staying close to the trees. Fifty yards later, dropping to both knees, he wrapped his left arm around Ayda's back. While shoving two fingers into a vest pocket, he lifted her torso.

Swallowing, her mouth opening and closing, the woman blinked repeatedly at him. Her right hand patted at his body before grabbing his muscle shirt.

Gaping at her, Jacob retrieved an inhaler and shook the device, his mind noticing her big, beautiful blue eyes.

"Be..." her chest heaving in vain, she twisted his shirt and pulled, "be..."

He glanced at the container and brought the medication to her lips.

Her body jerking, "...hind," the muscles in her neck showing through the skin, she smacked the inhaler out of Jacob's hand and, "...you," threw out her left arm.

Putting the fragmented words together, Jacob tensed, let go of Ayda, rolled to his right and thrust out his left boot, into a man's gut.

　　　　ABOVE & BEYOND

Cole doubled over. The pistol in his grasp discharged a round; a spray of sandy earth flew into the air.

Springing to his feet, Jacob clutched the man's gun hand and wrist. He pushed.

Cole shoved back.

A pirouetting dance developed, both men pushing and shoving, trying to gain control of the weapon. Several bullets flew into the night sky. The grapplers swung the gun downward. The semi-automatic fired. Two bullets skipped off the surface of the lake.

Jacob pumped his legs and drove his adversary toward the tree line.

Cole fought back and halted his rearward momentum. His trigger finger contracted; a projectile clipped a low-hanging branch.

Jacob lifted a knee into Cole's side, brought his leg back and delivered two more blows.

The gun fired and the slide locked back.

Jacob let go and reached for the Coonan under his left arm. His fingers closed around air. He shot a look at the empty holster before reaching for the Mossberg.

Cole swung the two-pound steel weight.

The muzzle smashing into the left side of his head, Jacob spun around, his arms flaring out to his sides. His legs wobbled before he fell to one knee.

Cole pounced. Getting Jacob in a chokehold, his feet spread wide, Cole locked his left fist into the crook of his other arm and squeezed.

On both knees, Jacob grabbed the man's elbow, lurched forward, and wrenched downward on the appendage.

Cole pulled back and increased his efforts to strangle his prey.

Jacob spotted Ayda. Her body-rocking spasms had become twitches. Her lips matched the color of her eyes, blue. He clenched his teeth. *She's dying.*

Cole twisted his opponent's neck.

Resisting the urge to free himself, Jacob eyed Ayda. *Hang on, sweetheart.* Grabbing the Mossberg's pistol grip with his right hand, he racked the downward-facing weapon with his free hand, angled the muzzle outward and worked the trigger with his right pinky.

A gritty, sandy, upward air wash hit the right side of his face a split-second after a deafening blast. The first round in the long gun had been frangible. The rest were double ought buckshot.

Cole bellowed. His grip on Jacob's throat loosened. Screaming, he staggered away, toward the trees, looking down at the remnant of his right foot, a stump.

Jumping to his feet, Jacob rumpled the crippled man's shirt. Cocking his right arm, he bashed Cole's face three times before planting a boot in the center of the man's chest and launching him backward.

Cole collided with a wide tree trunk. His arms fell to his sides. He stared at Jacob. A trickle of blood ran from the corner of his mouth. His gaze traveled to the branch protruding from his chest. The pointed end of the two-inch diameter limb was covered with his own blood. His legs giving out, the dying man slid down the bark a few inches before the wooden spike suspended his frame. Two seconds later, his head slumped to one side.

Jacob bolted toward Ayda. He fished out his flashlight and found the inhaler, a few feet away from her. Hugging her shoulders, "Ayda," he lifted her upper body, grabbed her chin and jostled her head. "Come on, Ayda. Stay with me."

Wheezing, Ayda blinked a couple times.

In his ear, Stockwell: "Jake, are you all right? I heard gunshots."

He pushed the inhaler between Ayda's lips and activated the device. Hearing Zoe's voice in his mind, he put his face next to Ayda's and held her head. "Breathe, Ayda, breathe. Just focus on getting that first breath."

Her eyelids drooped.

"Not going to happen, Ayda." He slapped her cheeks, shook the medication and reinserted the nozzle. "Come on, dear. Zoe wants to see her sister again."

Ayda's eyes opened a little more.

He spread his knees and acquired a better hold on her. "Give me one, Ayda."

She blinked and clutched his vest.

Jacob felt her dragging him down. "That's it. Fight. Fight for your life. Get that first breath." He pressed the button.

Stockwell: "Talk to me, Jake. What's going on?"

Ayda arched her back and drew in a short breath.

Jacob waited.

Her chest falling, she flicked her eyes toward him and gripped his hand, the one holding her medicine.

Feeling her pulling on the inhaler, he slid the plastic tip into her mouth and mashed the button again.

Ayda sucked in a longer, slower gulp of air. Seconds later, the muscles in her face relaxed and her left hand dropped to her stomach. After filling her lungs a few more times, she went limp, letting Jacob hold her.

He noticed the color return to her face and lips. Supporting her with his left arm, he cupped the back of her head with his right hand and kissed her forehead. "It's okay, sweetheart. It's okay. Just take it easy."

Ayda licked her lips. "Zo," her voice was weak, "Zo."

He frowned before nodding his head. "Zoe's fine. She's with my partner as we speak."

The spent woman sighed and rolled her head away from him.

"You had me worried there for a second."

She rotated her head back toward him. "Sor—" she wetted her lips and swallowed, "sorry about that."

He smiled. "I'm sorry too...that I didn't get here sooner." Cradling the Innocent, he looked across the lake. The moonlight reflected off the water's calm surface. A perfect breeze barely ruffled his hair. He tipped back his head and glimpsed the stars. *Under any other circumstances, this would be—*

"Jake!"

He righted his head. "We're good, Stockwell. Tell Zoe her sister's safe. We'll be there as soon as Ayda's ready to go." He heard a long, heavy sigh in his ear.

"Copy that. We're looking forward to seeing the two of you."

He lowered his gaze toward Ayda. "Thanks for the heads-up by the way." He motioned behind him, toward Cole. "He would have killed us both if you hadn't warned me."

She gave him a feeble smile and angled her hand away from her belly, aiming her thumb skyward. A second passed. "Who," she cleared her throat, "who are you?"

"I'm St. Christopher. But you can call me Jacob."

She half chuckled. "Considering you just," she took a big breath, "saved my life, I think I'll," she coughed, "I think I'll stick with calling you Saint Christopher."

He smiled. "That's just fine with me. Do you think you're ready to get up yet?"

"I'm a little worn out, but...I think I can walk."

He carefully laid her on the sandy ground, "Stay here," before leaving. Ten seconds later, he returned, holstering his 1911. He stooped and lifted her off the ground. "Well, lucky for you, Miss Gentry..."

She wrapped her arms around his neck.

Jacob carried her down the shoreline. "...you won't have to walk just yet."

1:26 A.M.

His lower legs dangling off the F-150's tailgate, Jacob winced when the medical technician dabbed the cut above his left eye. Stockwell had moved the Ford, parking the truck near the house, so the flood of emergency vehicles could get up the driveway.

In addition to an ambulance, several other vehicles, including state police cruisers—lights flashing—were parked on the property. An unmarked SUV pulled up beside the ambulance and emptied its passengers; one strode toward Jacob and Stockwell's pickup.

Sitting on his right, barely swinging her legs, Stockwell gave Jacob a sideways glance. "This ought to be fun."

He made a face at the oncoming figure. "I think we can take him."

She smiled at the side of her man's face. "Left and low?"

He inwardly laughed, his shoulders rocking a few times. "High and right." Jacob jutted out his chin at the FBI man. "Agent Williams...it's good to see you again."

The man stopped and put hands on his hips. After an intensive scan of the area, already knowing about the body count inside the cabin, he spied his female counterpart, "Agent Stockwell," and flicked his eyes to the right, "Jake."

Several awkward moments of staring and exchanging

looks passed among the agents.

Williams faced Stockwell. "This was my operation. I was in charge."

Jacob brushed aside the EMT's hand. "I made the call on this, Carter."

"Shut up, Jake." Williams pointed. "You're not with the bureau anymore. So I don't give a damn about what you have to say."

Jacob clenched fists and forearms. His chest muscles bounced upward.

Williams aimed the digit at Stockwell. "And you...you know the protocol, the chain of command. When you learned about," he waved the finger at the structure behind her, "*this*...you should have looped me in."

Stockwell nodded. "I apologize. It was time sensitive. We had to move quickly."

Returning his hand to his hip, Williams nodded back. "You're just lucky everything turned out the way it did." After pivoting his upper body left and right, looking around, "So where is," he faced forward, "Mr. Calvin Cole anyway?"

Jacob jerked a thumb over his shoulder. "He's hanging around in the woods."

Stockwell cranked her head around, toward the house, trying to conceal a short snigger.

Williams glimpsed her before frowning at her partner.

Jacob bobbed his head backward. "You'll see what I

mean when you get back there.”

After another drawn out visual exchange, Williams nodded again, “Stockwell…Jake,” and walked toward the rear of the property.

The EMT applied a butterfly bandage to Jacob’s wound and gathered his supplies. “You’re all set.”

“Hey,” Jacob motioned toward the ambulance, and Ayda and Zoe inside, “how are they doing?”

“I can’t disclose their medical information.”

Jacob held out his hands, palms up, encompassing the two female patients, and the woman beside him. “We’ve been through hell together. I don’t think they’ll mind.”

The EMT gave Ayda and Zoe a long look, sighed and faced the agents. “We’ve treated their immediate medical issues, but they should really see a doctor for a full physical…just as a precaution.” He aimed a finger at Jacob. “And that’s all I’m going to say on the matter. Anything else you’ll have to take up with *them*.”

“So they’re free to travel…we can take them home?”

“I don’t see why not.”

Jacob extended his right hand. “Thank you.”

The men exchanged handshakes.

Jacob pointed at his bandage. “And thanks for taking care of this too.”

“You’re welcome.” The EMT left.

Jacob jumped to the ground, spun around and stood in front of Stockwell.

She half grinned. “He’s hanging around in the

woods?"

Hearing his words from a minute ago, he let out a quick snicker. "That was a good one, wasn't it?" He placed flat hands on the tailgate, next to her outer thighs, and inclined toward her. "You were great tonight, you know that? Your aim was perfect. You saved Zoe's life."

"Hey," she looked around before sliding her hands off her pants and covering his fingertips with hers, "we both know this was a team effort."

He savored the beauty of her blue eyes in the moonlight. "We do make a good team."

Her mind envisioning the emergency personnel moving around about them, she leaned as close to him as she dared. "We make a *great* team, Mr. St. Christopher." She brushed the pads of her fingers back and forth over his nails. "Now let's get Ayda and Zoe home, so we can..." she puckered and lightly blew on his lips, "spend some time together...just you and me."

"Ooh, I like the sound of that; more teamwork." He glanced at her lap before meeting her gaze. "Maybe you can help me with my door-breaching technique."

Observing his deadpan expression for a few moments, she let a cascading grin overtake her poker face. "You're so cute when you throw out those sexual innuendos...or pretend to fumble with your words."

One corner of his lips nudged upward a hair.

"You know exactly what you're saying...all the time."

The second corner of his mouth mirrored the first.

"Am I that transparent?"

"Yes, but I love it." She shook her head. "Don't ever change."

Taking her hand, "Deal," he helped her off the tailgate and the two made their way to the ambulance, to Ayda and Zoe.

2:32 A.M.
WAPPINGERS FALLS
DUTCHESS COUNTY, NEW YORK

Jacob took the circular drive at the end of the court, stopping the F-150 at the curb in front of the Gentry's home. The same black Mercedes was parked in the driveway, backed up to the garage. This time, however, someone rushed out of the house.

Mrs. Gentry ran by the car, cutting across the lawn and heading straight for the Ford.

Stockwell had barely opened her door when the rear passenger door flew open.

Both Ayda and Zoe scrambled out of the truck and met their mother on the front lawn. Hugs and kisses were lavished on the daughters. The girls hugged and kissed their mother.

Stockwell pushed her door the rest of the way open and placed a boot on the running board.

Jacob caught her forearm. "Hold on a minute."

She turned back toward him.

He pointed his forehead at the family gathering. "This is my favorite part."

She observed the celebration.

His hand slid down to hers. "This makes all the

bumps, bruises and bloodied knuckles," he paused, "worth it."

Squeezing his hand, Stockwell pressed her back against the seat, butterflies stirring in her belly. She smiled. "Yes it does." A moment later, she recalled the trip here. Ayda and Zoe had inquired about their father. Stockwell and Jacob had said nothing. "Too bad," her voice was flat, "the happiness won't last for long."

Knowing what she was alluding to, he shot a look her way, "Our job is to rescue them from danger," before going back to the three-way embrace on the lawn. "Breaking bad news is," headlights drew his attention, "better left," he squinted at the rearview mirror, "to family members."

A car pulled up behind the agents. The lights went dark. The driver door swung outward.

Jacob glimpsed the male figure's reflection in the side-view mirror.

The newcomer crossed between the car and the F-150, emerging on the passenger side of the truck.

Jacob exited the Ford and met Stockwell at the right front corner of the pickup.

Ayda and Zoe shouted, "Uncle Al," and ran to meet the man in a black suit, black Oxfords and white, open-collar shirt.

Jacob leaned against the truck's fender.

Stockwell mimicked his posture.

He folded arms and crossed ankles.

She looked up at him.

He looked at her.

Both of them said, "Uncle Al?" simultaneously.

Ayda and Zoe hugged Higs nearly as hard as they had their mother.

. . .

After a prolonged greeting, the Gentry's and Higs approached the truck. Mrs. Gentry caught Jacob's eye, motioned to her right and ambled in the same direction.

He pushed away from the Ford and met her several feet ahead of the front bumper.

She pivoted toward him. "Thank you for keeping your promise."

"My pleasure, ma'am."

"Before you showed up," the woman clasped hands in front of her waist and regarded her children, "I honestly didn't think I'd ever see them again." She faced Jacob. "You renewed my faith...my hope. Thank you, Mr. St. Christopher. I'm sorry. *Jacob*."

He smiled. "You're very welcome."

"I think I already know the answer, but I have to ask." She glimpsed her kids and eyed their rescuer. "Have you told them...about their father?"

"No ma'am. That's something that needs to come from you."

Studying the pavement, "I'm," Mrs. Gentry fiddled with her interlaced fingers, rolling her thumbs a few times, "I'm not sure I know how to do that."

Jacob observed Ayda and Zoe, his mind recalling what the girls had shared during the drive, about their captivity. He put a hand on the back of Mrs. Gentry's upper arm. "Ma'am, your daughters are extremely resilient, tough women. I think the best approach is to be straight with them."

She observed him.

"I'm not saying the truth won't hurt, but..." he poked a finger at the freed women, "you've raised some strong kids. This won't ruin them."

She half smiled, "Thank you," and pivoted her head to see Ayda coming towards them. "I think I needed to hear that." Mrs. Gentry gazed at the man, who had kept his promise, brought her children home. "From the bottom of my heart, I hope you find your daughter, Mr. St. Christopher."

He nodded once. "Thank you."

"If there's *anything* I can ever do to help...please call me. I have money. And I have influential contacts."

"I appreciate the offer, ma'am."

"Hey Mom," Ayda pulled up short, "can I have a word with Jacob?"

"Of course, dear." After glimpsing him, her eyes extending another 'thank you,' Mrs. Gentry walked away.

Ayda watched her mother leave before facing her savior. "I never really got the chance to thank you for saving my life down by the water. Well, actually not just there," she waved her hands in the air, "the whole thing I mean."

"You're welcome, Ayda."

"That was the worst asthma attack I've ever had. I *literally* thought I was going to die. If you hadn't been there," her voice trailed off, as she turned her head and bit her lower lip, her mind taking her back to the scene, "I...I'm..." she emptied her lungs in one rush and came back to him. "Well, I guess I just wanted to thank you...properly."

He nodded.

"Okay," she let out another short breath, "I guess we should join the others."

They made their way to the group.

Zoe and Stockwell separated from a clinch. The elder woman rubbed Zoe's arm a few times. "I'm glad I could be there for you and your sister."

The identical twins crisscrossed in front of the agents.

Jacob thought he was seeing a human shell game, until he realized it was Zoe's arms around his neck. Embracing her, he felt her body tense and heard a groan in his ear. His eyes grew wide, as he envisioned the laceration he had covered with his shirt. "Oh man I'm sorry." He released her. "I forgot about your back."

"It's okay." Her chest heaved before she exhaled. "That'll heal. If it weren't for you...I'd be dead already."

Mrs. Gentry smiled at her daughters for several moments before standing taller. "Ay...Zo Zo, let's go inside." She gave Jacob a strained look. "There's something I need to tell you both."

He flashed a disappearing smile and offered the mother a quick nod.

After arching eyebrows at him and expelling a short sigh, she wrapped arms around her children and led them toward the house.

Anchoring the right flank of a semi-circle, with Stockwell in the middle, Higs watched the women walk across the lawn. "I do hope my presence here has not spoiled your enjoyment of the moment, Mr. St. Christopher." Higs knew how his employee loved to watch reuniting family members. "I mean no disrespect, but your phone call was not sufficient for me. I just had to," he regarded his adopted-in-spirit nieces, *"see for myself*...that they were indeed unharmed."

Jacob joined in watching Mrs. Gentry disappear into the house behind Ayda and Zoe. "I understand," he shifted his gaze toward the other man, *"Uncle Al."*

Stockwell sniggered.

Higs squinted at Jacob out of one eye. "As soon as they vocalized that name, I knew I would be hearing the moniker again...from *you.*"

His shoulders rocking, Jacob laughed. "And I think you might be hearing it a few more times too."

Higs smiled before his face went stoic. "Thank you," he panned left to include Stockwell, "both of you. You went *Above and Beyond* the call of duty on this assignment. You have my deepest, sincerest gratitude."

She reached out. "We were happy..."

Turning, he barely lifted his arms toward her.

Stockwell patted his upper arm, "...to help."

He quickly brought his hands together.

Noticing the truncated gesture, she took a step forward and initiated a hug.

Jacob nodded. "Anything for you, Higs."

After a brief hesitation, Higs returned her embrace. "Thank you, Ms. Stockwell." He backed away and retrieved his phone. "My intention is to remain here for a spell; however, before this slips my mind," he gave up the cell to Jacob, "it's your turn."

Jacob saw a digital photo of their chess game. "I thought you'd make that move." He gave the device to its owner. "Queen to King's Bishop seven. *Check*."

Higs studied the game pieces for several seconds. "And it would appear a 'mate' is in order as well." He scrutinized the taller man. "If I'm not mistaken, I seem to recall you telling me that you weren't very adept at the game of chess."

For several moments, Jacob showed no emotion before the corner of his mouth inched upward. "I've been playing since I was six."

Higs hiked his eyebrows.

"My father taught me. Three years later, I was winning on a regular basis. At sixteen, I entered a state tournament...and won."

Higs crossed arms over his chest and patted his lips.

"I was playing against people many years older than me," Jacob snorted, "even men with beards. I beat them all."

Higs wagged his finger at Jacob. "Mr. St. Christopher, you haven't been very forthright with me, regarding your talents."

"I think the correct word here is...*sandbagging*, Higs." Jacob chuckled. "I've been sandbagging. I couldn't resist the urge to mess with you a little."

Higs displayed a rare smile. "Well played, sir."

Jacob bowed a short ways and rolled a hand.

"A gentleman, however, offers his defeated opponent a rematch."

"Done...in fact, I think we should always have a game in play."

Higs nodded. "I'd like that." He eyed the house. "Now if you'll excuse me, I'm going to see if I can lend any assistance." He acknowledged his people, "Ms. Stockwell...Mr. St. Christopher," before striding across the lawn.

Jacob opened the F-150's passenger door and took Stockwell's hand.

She climbed into the truck. "Thank you."

"I feel like we've done this already, except..." he ran an index finger over the air above her pant legs, "I believe I saw *skin* here before."

She held his cheek. "And you will again."

Chuckling, he shut her door, walked around the Ford's front bumper and sat behind the steering wheel. "I just had an idea." He buckled his seatbelt and adjusted the shoulder harness. "How about we get dressed up and I'll take you someplace nice. And when I say 'dressed up' I mean," he jabbed his thumb toward the roof a couple times, "*up...up.*"

"That sounds great. I'll wear my..."

He rotated the ignition switch.

"...best polyester pants."

Stopping short of starting the vehicle, he pivoted his head toward her, the dashboard lights illuminating his sulking face.

Stockwell beamed. "Kidding...just kidding."

Matching her expression, he added a slow headshake and started the engine.

July 27TH; 11:37 A.M.
NEW YORK CITY

After leaving the Gentry's home, Jacob and Stockwell had holed up in his house for the next fifty-seven hours, enjoying some downtime, catching up on sleep, lounging around and playing a couple video games. Today, they were tying up loose ends.

The apartment door opened and a smiling Morgan filled the doorway. "Mr. St. Christopher...Agent Stockwell."

Jacob and Stockwell mimicked the man's facial expression and replied, "Hello Morgan."

The man backed away and pivoted. "Please come in."

Ahead of her partner, Stockwell entered the minimalist one-bedroom dwelling; a loveseat on the left, a simple chair against the far wall—a small table next to it. Hanging on the right wall, a 32-inch television rounded out the main living space. Looking left, glimpsing the kitchen area a few feet away, on the other side of the loveseat, she noted a microwave, a few utensils and one pot and one frying pan.

After closing the door, Morgan stood in front of the

TV, facing his visitors. "I can't thank you two enough for everything you've done. I couldn't believe my ears when the manager told me I was hired."

Stockwell smiled. "That's great news."

"Please thank Mr. Higginbottom for me." Upon learning of Morgan's situation from Jacob, Higs had made a phone call and obtained for Morgan an interview with a tech company in New York City. He also secured the apartment for Morgan and Samuel, paying for six-months of rent up front and giving the man a small sum of cash to get him through until his first paycheck arrived. "I thanked him over the phone, but I'd appreciate it if you would pass on my sentiments again."

Jacob nodded. "We will." He crossed his arms and looked up at the big man. "So when do you start?"

"Next week. The company," he lifted hands and glanced around, "gave me a few days to get settled into my new place. Care for the grand tour?" Not waiting for a reply, he plodded ahead, pumping open hands downward, "this is the living room," he pointed beyond Stockwell's shoulder, "kitchen," and jabbed his thumb over his shoulder, "bedroom and bathroom." He grinned. "And that concludes the tour."

The agents laughed.

"I'm kidding. Sam and I love our new home. Compared to sleeping in a van," he admired the apartment, "this place is like a fancy hotel."

Stockwell glimpsed the bedroom door. "So where *is*

Samuel anyway? I was looking forward to seeing him again."

"There's a nice woman in the building with a son Samuel's age. She's agreed to watch Sam, while I'm working...until I can find permanent day care." Morgan checked his watch. "Actually, I'll be picking him up in a few minutes." He observed his guests. "Can you stay for lunch? I know Sam would love to see you."

Jacob spied his timepiece and gawked at Stockwell for a few seconds.

She dipped her forehead toward him. "It's your call. You're the one making plans for tonight."

Thinking of the evening's upcoming events, he gave her a quick smile before nodding once at Morgan. "I think we can stay for a bit."

. . .

5:41 P.M.
CLARKSTOWN, NEW YORK

After slipping her foot into the four-inch, black suede ankle-strap high heel, Stockwell stood straight and pivoted both ways, examining herself in the full-length mirror. She smiled before half closing an eye at her hair, tied loosely on top of her head with a black ribbon. She pulled out the satin strip, shook her hair free and added volume with her fingers.

After another ten seconds of deliberation, she put her hair up and tied the ribbon again. Scooping a pair of earrings off the dresser and slinging a black clutch purse over one shoulder, she hurried out of her room. "Okay

Jake...I'm ready." Her head off to one side, her fingers fumbling near her earlobe, she walked into the living room; it was empty. "Jake?"

After checking the kitchen, she strolled back down the hall, while securing her second earring. Poking her head into his bedroom, "Jake?" she quickly scanned the area. The doorbell rang and she spun around, her eyebrows coming together.

Stockwell moved as fast as she could in the deep purple, long-sleeved, curve-hugging dress, and spiked heels. Stopping to peek out the front window, she spotted Jacob's Mustang parked in the driveway. *He has to be here somewhere.*

Grabbing the doorknob, she put an eye to the peephole. A smile forming on her face, she opened the door and gave the man in a black suit and black shoes, white shirt and dark purple tie the once-over.

Holding flowers in his hands, Jacob opened his mouth, but no words escaped. Starting at her heels, his eyes moved upward—shapely legs in black nylons disappeared under her tight-fitting dress's hem, which stopped three inches above the knee. Above smooth, rounded breasts and beneath the dress's mock neck, a see-through black, lace floral panel spread across her upper chest before running down each sleeve.

A flower slipped from his hand and landed on his shoe.

After a quick look down, he stooped, gathered the

stray, red rose and stood tall again. "Wow."

Still clutching the doorknob with her left hand, Stockwell threw out her right hip and put her free hand on her waist. "What are you doing, ringing the doorbell? This is *your* house, silly."

"Well," he admired her sexy pose, "I..." before focusing on her blue eyes, full and dark lashes, "I..." he blinked a few times, "I'm picking you up for our date." He held out the bouquet. "I even brought flowers."

She took them and put her nose to the roses. After a short sniff, she looked at her wet hand. "Wait." She half turned her upper body and gestured toward the living room, "Aren't these the ones from..." before pivoting back and seeing him holding a shrug.

"I'm winging it here." He rolled both hands. "Just go with the flow, Stockwell."

She laughed. "I love them...thank you." She kissed him and motioned behind her, her mind envisioning the empty vase in the living room. "In fact, I have the *perfect place* for them."

He chuckled and nodded. "Very funny."

Stockwell walked back into the house and returned, empty-handed. "So are we ready?"

"Almost." He drew nearer to her, wrapped arms around her shoulders and undid the black ribbon holding her hair in place.

Her locks fell.

He used his fingers as a comb before sinking them

deeper into her mane, holding her head and giving her a long kiss. Jacob pulled his lips away from hers.

Stockwell caught her breath.

He regarded her earrings—a purple amethyst stone dangling at the end of a long, tiny gold chain—before he brushed a stray tuft of hair away from her face. "Now we're ready."

. . .

7:02 P.M.
NEW YORK CITY

Jacob pushed in Stockwell's chair, as she sat.

"Thank you." She situated herself on the cane-backed chair's round, wine-colored seat, while pulling down the hem of her dress. She glanced around. "I can't believe places like this still exist."

Jacob claimed his chair across from her and joined her in taking in the room's ambience.

Four chandeliers, strategically placed around the ballroom, supplied subdued lighting. Around three of the four outside walls, three rows deep, round bistro tables for two set the mood for intimacy. Anchored to the walls were various paintings and sculptures.

A live band—the members dressed in black suits and white shirts—played on an elevated stage near the fourth outside wall. Large speakers were hidden in the room's dark corners. In the center of the room was the dance floor.

"This place just opened up a month ago." Jacob eyed his date for the evening. "Do you like it?"

She crossed her legs under the table. "I love it." After surveying the room again, she leaned closer to him. "I feel like I'm a teenager again."

He looked at her. "What do you mean?"

She cocked her head toward the other patrons. "Age wise?"

After another inspection of the room, he nodded. "True." Outside of one couple, in their early twenties, the rest of the people were all over fifty years old; most were approaching their sixth decade. He glimpsed her dress. "So what you're telling me is...it wouldn't mean as much to you if I were to say...you're the hottest woman here?"

She smiled. "Well I don't know. Let's find out."

Matching her expression, he slid his hand across the table, "Deanna," and held hers, "You're the most beautiful woman here."

Her heart rate rising, she beamed. "I guess you were wrong. It still meant a lot to me. Thank you."

He chuckled.

She spied his dark purple tie. "By the way," she pointed her chin toward the narrow apparel, "nice choice on the tie."

He looked down and came back to her. "I had a hunch you might be wearing something complementary." Purple was Stockwell's favorite color.

She snickered, took a drink of water and watched the couples in the middle of the room, slow dancing. "So why did you choose this place?"

"You said you wanted to date me, get to know me, find out what I like and don't like."

Her eyebrows traveled higher. "Are you telling me you like dancing?" She tipped her head toward the performers, "*Slow* dancing?"

"I'd like anything," he ogled her attire, "if it gets you to dress like that."

Feeling her chest getting warmer, she smiled and turned away, toying with her earring.

He spent the next half-minute admiring her. Stockwell watched people pirouette around the floor.

He took her hand. "Would you like to dance?"

Facing him, she uncrossed her legs. "I'd love to."

Jacob escorted her to an open spot, near the band.

She turned toward him. "I must be honest with you. Even though I like to dance...I'm not as good as I used to be when I was a kid. And I only remember a few dances."

He took her right hand in his left, curled his free arm around her waist and gently pulled her to himself. "Do you know how to waltz?"

She placed her left hand on his right shoulder. "I do."

"Then let's go with that. You ready?"

Smiling, she nodded.

Jacob stepped forward with his left foot and out with his right, while Stockwell went back with her right foot and out with her left. They brought their feet together and Jacob started the next forward step with his right foot, Stockwell her left. They repeated the moves, making a small circle in their corner of the floor.

Stockwell smiled. "You're really good."

"Only when I have the right partner." His gaze dipped to her dress. "Excuse me. Only when I have a...*sexy*...partner."

She chuckled.

A minute later, the music ended and they separated. Stockwell took his hand, "That was fun," and led him toward their table.

A voice from the speakers: "All right, ladies and gentlemen...now we're going to speed things up a little with...an Argentine Tango."

Jacob pulled Stockwell's hand.

She spun back toward him.

He embraced her, his eyes wide.

Arching her back, her long hair hanging a few inches away from her body, she regarded him for a moment before her eyes matched his in size. She slowly shook her head. "Jake, I haven't done the Argentine Tango in years."

"Do you know the basic eight?"

"I think so...but I always get my feet twisted up during the windmill."

The music started.

Jacob shuffled backward, onto his right foot, "Can you do ochos?" before sliding left, onto his left foot.

Stockwell followed him. "I think I remember."

He came to position five in the dance and stopped. "Go for it."

She stepped left with her right foot, swiveled around on that shoe and stepped back to her original position, leading with her left foot. After repeating the moves, she stood in front of her dance partner, her feet crossed at the ankles. She lifted her eyes to meet his. "I did it."

"I had no doubts, Stockwell. Now...are you ready to show me one of those sexy, high leg kicks we talked about?"

She half smiled. "You're calling my bluff, aren't you?"

Mimicking her, he nodded. "Uh-huh."

She chuckled. "You win then."

Making sure she noticed him, Jacob gave her outfit an admiring look before coming back to her. "You're right. I feel like I won the jackpot tonight."

Smiling, batting eyelashes, she averted her gaze.

They finished the last three steps, completing the square.

Stockwell brought her high heels together. "I stand corrected. You're a *great* dancer."

"I'll let you in on a little secret." Taking her with him, he glided backward and to his left. Her breasts pressed firmly against his pectoral muscles, he held her tightly to himself. The two dancer's right thighs grazed each other, as their legs and feet carried them through the steps.

Three.

Four.

Five.

Jacob stopped.

Stockwell crossed her ankles.

He guided her into a slight pivot. "The key to slow dancing is…"

She uncrossed her feet.

"…no separation…" he led her through the ochos and drew her close again, "…two people, a man and a woman, becoming," he peered into her blue eyes, "*one*…with their bodies."

Their front halves commingling, their heads offset, they gazed at one another, she up and to her right, he down and to his right, their chins nearly touching.

Breathing a tad heavier, her eyes darting up and down—from his eyes to his lips—Stockwell felt a rush of heat spread over her chest and up her neck. "I certainly like," her chest expanded a little, "the sound of that."

Six.

Seven.

Eight.

The couple stopped at their starting position.

She tipped her head back. "But somehow I…" her mouth opened a sliver.

Jacob spied the tip of her tongue, peeking out and moving across her lilac-colored lips a fraction of an inch. He dipped his head and kissed her, softly and slowly, before pulling back a short ways.

"Somehow," she drew in a breath, "I get the feeling you're not just talking about," she arched an eyebrow, "*dancing*, are you?"

A mischievous grin on his face, "Miss Stockwell..." Jacob moved backward, taking her with him.

One.

Two.

"...you're as wise..."

Three.

Four.

Five.

"...as you are beautiful."

She stopped and crossed her ankles. "Why thank you, Mr. St. Christopher."

He led her into forward ochos.

She executed the moves and came back into his arms.

Six.

Seven.

Eight.

Back at the starting position, no space between him and his partner, Jacob lifted one corner of his mouth, a gleam in his eye. "You ready for a windmill now?" Bringing her with him, to the first position, he felt her body tense.

"I don't know, Jake. I might trip."

He ushered her to the second position. "Trust me. I've got strong arms."

"I don't want to fall."

Three.

Four.

"You won't." He stopped at number five. "Just follow

my lead." He steered her into a slight turn, so she could uncross her feet. "Right foot first…"

Like going from home plate to third base, she took one stride to her left with her right foot, and brought her high heels together.

"…turn right and step to the side with your…"

She made a ninety-degree right turn and took another step, leading with her left foot.

Like a baseball pitcher, standing on the mound, "That's it," Jacob spun to his right.

Bringing her feet together, she did a clockwise one-eighty, and moved backward onto her right foot, toward first base.

Jacob pivoted with her. "You got it."

She beamed from ear to ear.

"Bring it home, Stockwell."

She strode to her left, back to her original position.

He caught her eye. "Ochos?"

Smiling, panting, her heart beating faster, she nodded once. "You know it." She performed the moves, this time adding a backward kick after each foot swivel.

Jacob laughed.

Stockwell giggled.

Six.

Seven.

Eight.

The music stopped. Clapping started.

Jacob wiped his forehead. Stockwell fanned herself

with both hands. The duo looked around. They were the only ones on the floor. He hugged his woman and kissed her on the cheek before the couple made their way to their table, each with an arm around the other's waist.

She spied his darkening face. "It looks like someone's a little embarrassed."

"No," he pinched his shirt and repeatedly tugged on the garment, forcing cool air inside, "it's just warm in here."

She grinned. "Or maybe you're just a hot dancer."

He let out a short laugh. "Yeah, I'm sure that's it."

. . .

11:27 P.M.
CLARKSTOWN, NEW YORK

Following a light meal and more dancing, Jacob and Stockwell had taken a long walk around New York City before driving back to his house.

Standing outside her bedroom, his arms around her waist, her arms around his neck—her wrists crossed, high heels dangling from two curled fingers—Jacob and Stockwell enjoyed a long kiss before they separated.

She lowered herself to her pantyhose-clad feet. "I had a great time tonight."

He gently caressed her lower back. "Me too."

"I honestly can't remember the last time I cut loose like that and just...had fun. Thank you."

"You're welcome." He lifted his wrist and spied the time over her shoulder. "And look...I even had you home by eleven-thirty." He came back to her. "Your dad would be pleased."

She let out a short snigger before glancing backward, into her room. "I'd invite you in..."

He arched his eyebrows.

"...but not on the first date."

Exaggerating the act as much as he could, he let his shoulders sag.

She smiled and put a hand to his cheek. "You poor thing."

"Any clues as to when that invitation might be extended?"

"A girl has to leave *some things* to the imagination."

He grinned before going in for a quick peck. "Good night, Deanna."

"Good night."

"I love you."

"I love you too, Jake."

He hesitated. "We should do this again...soon."

She rose to her tiptoes and kissed him, "Definitely," before backing into her room, while showing him a palm. "Good night."

He lifted his hand a short ways. "Good night."

Stockwell closed the door, tossed her shoes onto the floor and wandered toward the bed. She did a three-quarter spin and flopped onto the bed, arms spread wide, a broad grin on her face. A moment later, she frowned. *Did I just twirl around...like some...lovesick schoolgirl?*

Snickering to herself, she crawled under the covers,

still wearing her dress. She rolled onto her side, fluffed her pillow and found a comfortable spot for her head. Lowering her chin to her chest and pulling up on her dress, she breathed deeply the scent of Jacob's spiced aftershave.

. . .

Wearing sweatpants, Jacob climbed into bed and drew the covers up to his bare chest. He dropped his head onto the pillow and put interlaced fingers behind his head. Eyes wide, his heart still racing, he watched the ceiling fan overhead for a few minutes before glancing at the clock on the nightstand—11:58.

Shifting his focus back to the slow-moving fan, he tried following one, individual moving blade, his mind replaying the evening...

> *Stockwell did a clockwise one-eighty and moved backward onto her right foot.*
> *Remaining in place, Jacob pivoted with her. "You got it."*
> *She beamed from ear to ear.*
> *"Bring it home, Stockwell."*
> *She strode to her left, back to her original position. He caught her eye. "Ochos?"*
> *Smiling, panting, her heart beating faster, she nodded once. "You know it." She performed the moves, this time adding a backward kick after each foot swivel.*

Jacob laughed. *What a woman.* Several minutes passed

before he rolled onto his right side and brought the covers up higher. After another look at the clock—12:11—he closed his eyes, knowing sleep would be hard to come by tonight.

— **Thank You** —

Thank you for purchasing and reading *Above &*
Beyond. I hope you enjoyed this hostage rescue thriller.

Keep reading for a sneak peek at *Hard Road to*
Redemption, the fifth—and possibly the most powerful—
book in the Jacob St. Christopher series.

Blessings and Peace,

Alex

P.S. Don't forget your FREE ebook, *Escape & Evade*,
at my website (AlexAnderNovelist.com).

HARD ROAD TO
REDEMPTION

A HOSTAGE RESCUE THRILLER

ALEX
ANDER

CHAPTER 1
SPRINTERS

Bumper to bumper, the two unmarked, black Dodge Sprinters pulled up to a pair of side-by-side chain-link gates located in the middle of nowhere. Three-foot-square and eight-foot-high brick pillars—one on either side of the entry point—served as anchors for each gate. Ten-foot-wide sections of fencing—the same height as the pillars—extended laterally away from the brick columns. Eleven feet out, the fencing disappeared into the surrounding pitch-black, dense forest.

Holding an AR-15 decked out with sighting and illumination attachments, a man approached the lead van while rolling a finger in the air.

The driver lowered his window and acknowledged the armed man with a backward flip of his head. "Hell of a—" he swiped at the bugs trying to sneak into his space, "hell of a night, isn't it? How you live in this heat is beyond me."

AR slid a hand under the rifle sling around his neck and rubbed away the sweat building up on his skin. "You get used to it for the most part. But," he leaned back and shot a look at the sky, "on nights like these," before coming back to the visitor, "all you can think about is a cold beer and a *cool* shower."

The driver laughed. "I hear you, brother." He jerked a thumb over his shoulder. "Delivery. My boss is here with me. He wants to meet with *your* boss."

AR motioned toward his partner.

The second sentry worked a lock, unwound a chain, and pushed open one gate.

Like a cop directing traffic, AR waved the transports through and dug out a walkie-talkie. "I'll radio ahead and let them know you're coming."

"Thanks, man." After slapping the outside of his door twice and pointing at AR, "I hope you get that beer and shower soon," the driver eased the Sprinter by the guard opening the second gate.

. . .

His hands at ten and two o'clock on the Toyota Corolla's steering wheel, thirty-year-old Dexter Childress passed by the tree-lined dirt road he had watched the Dodge Sprinters drive down thirty seconds earlier. He threw a glance out the window on his left.

Brake lights shone back at him.

Headlights lit up a chain-link fence.

Men with rifles patrolled the area.

One of the armed men opened the gate while another motioned for the vehicles to go through.

Childress kept his foot on the accelerator.

A quarter mile later, spotting a hidden trail to his left—just wide enough to accommodate his Corolla—he drove the car off the road and onto the trail.

The reporter navigated the winding path, leaves and branches brushing against the rental car. He winced when he heard a twig drag across the length of the passenger door before he had time to crank the steering wheel to the left. *That'll drive up the cost of this assignment.*

A hundred yards later, the forest swallowed up the path.

He ran the gearshift to 'park' and shut off the ignition. The automatic headlights remained on. He pulled on a handle and shoved open his door.

The panel moved a foot and smacked against a tree.

He cursed while grabbing his high-powered digital camera and a backpack. "Oh yes. The," he squeezed shoulders through the narrow gap, "glamorous life of," before uncoiling the rest of his six-two, one-fifty skinny frame from the compact car, "an investigative reporter."

Wearing jeans and a dark-colored polo shirt, Childress eased the door shut, producing only a soft 'click' when the latch caught. He slung his pack and looked back the way he had come. Drawing an index finger through the air, left to right, he calculated the destination of the vans and set off in that direction.

. . .

The Sprinters stopped just inside a second set of

gates that joined with an eight-foot-high fence that encircled a sprawling compound of buildings. Their rear and side doors flew open, and each dodge disgorged four armed men in black tactical clothing and vests laden with spare magazines.

Performing a maneuver, one they had rehearsed dozens, maybe hundreds, of times before, the eight men fanned out and took defensive positions at the corners of the vans, each man shouldering an AR-15 at the low-ready position, his body squared with his area of responsibility—either a cardinal direction (north, east, south, west) or an ordinal direction (northeast, southeast, southwest, northwest).

Both drivers, and the lead vehicle's passenger, hopped out and swarmed at the second van's passenger door. All the operators carried a Knights Armament SR-30 M-LOK rifle chambered in 300 AAC Blackout and sporting a 9.5-inch barrel. One man pulled on the van's door handle.

Thirty-nine, exhibiting a short and dark, neatly trimmed mustache and beard, a man in blue jeans and a white, short-sleeve polo shirt slid out of his seat, his black tactical boots crunching gravel when his feet touched down. The six-foot man planted hands on hips and glanced around the area.

The largest structure—two stories high—was furthest away from the gate and dwarfed the many buildings dotting the landscape, which consisted of mostly matted earth with patches of grass here and there.

In the center of the compound was a playground of homemade toys and climbing apparatuses.

At the corners, where the fencing made ninety-degree turns, tall poles supported inward-facing spotlights, which were off.

Shorter poles, near the buildings, buoyed downward-facing, lower-intensity lights; most were off. Those that were on gave off enough light to make out most everything inside the perimeter fencing. Beyond that, thick trees provided a black backdrop.

Six-Foot leaned into the van and emerged a beat later with a cigarette and a cheap plastic lighter. He lit the cancer stick, took a drag, and tossed the lighter onto his seat. "These people live like backwoods hicks."

The man who had engaged in conversation with the guard at the main gate nodded while observing what his boss was seeing. "I couldn't agree more."

"But," Six-Foot chuckled, slammed the door, and headed for the two-story main house, "these hicks pay handsomely."

The three bodyguards suppressed sniggers while falling into flanking positions on Six-Foot's nine, twelve, and three o'clock.

"And for that," eyeing a gray-haired man emerging from the main house and striding toward him, Six-Foot drew more nicotine into his lungs and blew out a cloud of smoke that hung in the moist air, "I shall keep my opinions to myself." He slapped his neck, "Mother…" then ogled the remains of an insect. "Let's make this deal and get the," he cursed while wiping the dirty hand on his pants, "out of here."

. . .

From behind a pine tree located ten feet outside the compound's fence, Dexter Childress held down a button on his camera to zoom in on two individuals surrounded by heavily armed men.

A six-foot-tall man and an older, gray-haired man stood face-to-face, talking. A minute later, Gray Hair beckoned, and another man entered the circle of guns, a duffle bag in his grasp.

Six-Foot unzipped the bag, peered inside, and nodded before running the zipper again. He slung the duffle and shook hands with Gray Hair.

Gray Hair looked over his shoulder and motioned.

Several men jogged toward the Dodge Sprinters and jumped into the vehicles. Seconds later, they stepped out, each two-man team hefting a black carrying case. The teams stacked the cases and went back for more.

Childress snapped photo after photo of the activity, including several close-ups of Six-Foot and Gray Hair. The investigative reporter froze when his ears picked up a sound coming from his right.

Boots scuffing the ground accompanied heavy panting.

He pivoted his head, and a curse word flashed across

his mind. Crouching, he picked up his pack and backed away from his hiding spot, taking extra care to avoid stepping on any brittle twigs.

Fifteen paces later, he ducked behind a wide oak situated twenty feet away from the fence.

The scuffing boots and heavy panting grew louder.

Childress peeked out from behind the oak's trunk.

An armed sentry walked a black-and-brown-colored Doberman pinscher along the fence line.

The animal's ears went skyward. Growling, the dog lunged toward the fence.

The man tugged on the leash. "What is it, boy? What do you see?"

The guard dog barked twice before rising onto its rear legs and pulling the leash taut.

His back to the oak, repeating the same curse over and over in his mind, Childress shut his eyes. He made a face a tick later. *Can they shoot unarmed trespassers in this state?* He shook his head. *I'm sure you can shoot anyone for any reason and let the courts sort it out later.*

The pinscher barked.

The reporter huffed to himself. *Doesn't exactly help the dead guy, though, does it?*

The pinscher growled.

Off to his left, Childress noticed something in the underbrush. He squinted.

That something moved.

He frowned while recalling the contents of the

backpack at his feet. *What have I got to lose?*

. . .

Gray Hair unclipped the walkie-talkie from his belt and thumbed a button. "This is Colonel Hendricks. What's going on over there?" Hendricks let go of the button and observed the surrounding men.

Their postures had changed. Their rifles were pressed deeper into their shoulders, and the looks on their faces had become stoic.

Hendricks met Six-Foot's gaze and shook his head. "Don't worry, Mister Hunter. I'm sure it's nothing."

. . .

Seeing a flashlight beam coming from his six o'clock and illuminating the surrounding forest, Childress clenched in his left hand a double 'A' battery he had slipped from his pack.

The Doberman barked.

The beam of light panned to the right.

Childress tossed the battery to his left.

The power source landed and bounced twice, disturbing the pine needles covering the forest floor.

The light beam zipped to the left.

Snorting, a small, wild hog burst out of the underbrush and ran off.

The sentry watched the animal until the feral swine reached the limit of his flashlight's beam. He jerked the still barking Doberman away from the fence and thumbed his walkie-talkie. "It's just a pig." He strode along the fence line while occasionally yanking on the excited dog's leash. "The perimeter is secure."

Childress let out the air he had been holding while touching his head to the tree trunk behind him. Peeping over his right shoulder, he watched the guard, and the guard dog, make a right-hand ninety and walk toward the gate.

A few minutes passed, and he resumed taking pictures.

Six-Foot and Gray Hair shook hands.

The armed men and Six-Foot climbed into the vans.

The Sprinters turned around and drove through the gates, crossing paths with a beat-up minivan.

Two men got out of the minivan. The one on the passenger side slid open the side door.

A thin girl stumbled out of the vehicle.

Each man grasped one of her elbows then escorted the girl to a small building in front of the main house. All three went inside.

Childress sneaked away from the fence, returned to his car, and drove the Toyota, in reverse, all the way to the main road.